How I Met You

How I Met You

Stories by

Bradley Jay Owens

BRIGHT
HORSE
BOOKS

Brighthorse Books
13202 N River Drive
Omaha, NE 68112
brighthorsebooks.com

ISBN: 978-1-944467-09-8

Cover Photo © Page Light Studios
Author Photo © James Marsh

"A Circle of Stones" first appeared in *Ploughshares*; "Liebfraumilch" in *Folio*; "The Drowned" in slightly different form in *Henfield Prize Stories* (Warner Books, 1992); "The Christmas Cathedral" in *The Threepenny Review*; and "My Mother, Sewing" in *Fourteen Hills: SFSU Review*.

Brighthorse books are distributed to the trade through Ingram Book Group and its distribution partners. For more information, go to https://ipage.ingramcontent.com/ipage/li001.jsp. For information about Brighthorse Books, go to brighthorsebooks.com. For information about the Brighthorse Prize, go to https://brighthorsebooks.submittable.com/submit.

For Nora, who told me stories,
and for Barbara, who gave me books

"I cried because I had no shoes,
until I met a man who had no feet."

—homily on the wall of
Sutphen's Bar-B-Que Restaurant,
Amarillo, Texas

CONTENTS

A Circle of Stones

IN 1967, WHEN I was ten years old, my mother married Harlan Frame, and we moved that summer to a house he'd bought for us in Slaughter, Texas.

Harlan was a farmer, a word my mother found too plain; she'd tell people Harlan ranched, though he kept fewer than a dozen cows on a patch of scrub land that was too poor to support a crop. Mostly he farmed wheat and cotton. He would put some acres into sorghum if he thought a booming cattle market might push up the price of feed, but he called sorghum his casino crop because if he guessed wrong he'd lose what he put into it. It was not like wheat or cotton, he said, where insurance and the government made sure the farmer didn't get too badly hurt.

My mother could have done a whole lot worse than Harlan, and probably would have, given half a chance. As far as I know, Harlan is the only man who ever courted her, besides my father. Harlan overlooked the fact that she was divorced and had a child, which was to his credit. In the 1960s such things mattered more than they do now. Also, my mother was a knockout. She had pale blue eyes and dark hair, and she kept herself thin by eating only every other day. If Harlan hadn't come along, someone else would have, and then who knows where we'd have been? Worse off, most likely. My mother was easy prey for the unscrupulous because she believed herself to be more knowing than she was. Harlan Frame was the first man, after my father, who asked to marry her, and she said yes.

I felt no regret or hesitation about leaving Amarillo, where I'd grown up, for a farm town where I didn't know a soul. The apartment my mother and I shared was in an ugly duplex set at one end of a parking lot, in a part of Amarillo where there seemed to be a murder, rape, child-snatching, or assault a week. The man who lived behind us sometimes got drunk at night and argued violently with his wife, and a few times I'd awakened to the sound of someone quietly turning the knob of our front door, trying to get in. When that happened, Mother would call the police, and we'd lock ourselves inside the bathroom until they came.

I thought that one bad chapter in our lives was ending, and that we would start off fresh in Slaughter and have something like a normal life again.

•

THE HOUSE WE MOVED into had been neglected, and Harlan had to have the roof patched and the outside painted. Mother stripped the bedroom walls of old wallpaper and painted her room mint green and mine yellow. She lined the kitchen shelves and drawers with new tack paper, put new curtains up, and cleaned the pinewood paneling and cabinets with lemon oil. She and I spent all of one day cleaning windows with potato halves and crumpled pages from the newspaper, a method she'd learned from some women's magazine she'd picked up in the beauty parlor.

"Carpet," she said, bending down and squinting through the pane of glass I'd just cleaned. "That's the next priority." Then she straightened and gave me a quick, appraising look; I imagined I was being added to her list of items that could bear sprucing up. "Well," she said, crumpling another sheet of newspaper, "Rome wasn't built in a day."

I had never seen my mother work as hard as she worked on that house. In the three years since my father left, she had taken on the habits of an invalid, staying in her bathrobe all day, sleeping in the afternoon. She complained of feeling worn out, and would sometimes lapse into silences that could go on for days. Now she was a different person, energetic and determined, as if she'd left that old self behind, for good. We had done without for too long, she said, and now she meant to make up for it.

"I was young and stupid when your dad and I got married," she said. "What we've got here is a second chance."

•

MY FATHER GOT INTERESTED in visitation rights about the time we moved to Slaughter. By the terms of the divorce, he'd always had the right to see me two weekends a month, but he had rarely claimed the privilege. I saw him over Christmas or Thanksgiving and the few times he showed up on impulse at the duplex, saying that he wanted us to be a family again. He broke down the front door one time when my mother wouldn't let him in, and when he asked me if I wanted to come live with him, I said I did. We spent two days in the Starlight Motel in San Angelo, swimming in the motel pool and having food delivered to our room. When he brought me home, a sheriff's deputy was parked in front of our apartment, waiting.

My mother asked if I was all right, and I told her yes. Then she slapped me, hard, across the face. "That's for worrying me to death," she said.

When we moved to Slaughter, I hadn't seen my father in a year.

He called the second week we were down there. It was the first time we had heard our new phone ring, and I happened to be standing next to it. I picked it up.

"Hey, tiger," he said. "How's the new digs?"

I was too surprised, at first, to say a word. Finally, I said, "Hi, Dad," and that caught Mother's ear. She took the phone away and told me to go wait outside.

When I came back in, ten minutes later, she was grimly polishing a coffee urn, using toothpaste and old panty hose. She knew I was waiting, but she kept on like I wasn't there.

"Well?" I asked, at last.

She set the coffee urn down and turned to look at me. I could see the faint lines that the conversation with my father had brought out around her mouth and eyes. "Weekend after next," she said, "you're going to go see your father. You can ride the bus to Amarillo; he'll be there to meet you."

•

HARLAN WAS AN ONLY child. The fact that he had married a divorcée broke his widowed mother's heart, and she cut off contact with him. Mother and I would see Mrs. Frame creeping down our street in her green Valiant, wearing white gloves and a feathered hat. She'd let the car drift to the wrong side of the road as she leaned across the front seat to gape at the house. Mother kept the blinds closed so she couldn't see inside.

"That woman's going to have an accident," Mother would say. "Or cause one."

I spent most days inside, out of the heat, watching TV or reading. Harlan left early in the morning and stayed gone until suppertime; the land he farmed was twenty miles away, too far to be driving into town for lunch when there was cotton to be stripped, and winter wheat to get into the ground.

Sometimes I'd stand in the window in the living room and look out on the street. Nothing moved on still days but the heat waves shimmering above the asphalt; other days there would be dust storms. Inside the house, on those days, I would hear the wind throw sand against the house like it was rain.

One afternoon, when I was standing in the window, Mrs. Frame drove by. She lifted one white-gloved hand off the wheel and wiggled her fingers at me, tentatively, as if she were afraid the gesture might provoke me. I waved back.

Mother and I would go downtown for groceries twice a week, and we'd stop at the library to get more books. Her tastes ran to John Steinbeck and Harold Robbins, while I liked ghost stories and anything to do with flying saucers, the Bermuda Triangle, or the Loch Ness Monster. Slaughter didn't offer much else in the way of entertainment: there was one movie theater that played the same movie for a month at a time, and a bowling alley that was only open in the winter. There was a pretty green park downtown, lush with walnut trees and cottonwoods, that had a fishing pond, two bison penned up in a corral, and a "Whites Only" swimming pool. When integration came, in 1964, the town fathers had the pool drained rather than let Negroes use it, and in 1967 it was still shut down. If we got tired of being in the house, we'd go for a drive, and maybe stop at May's Drive-In for lime Cokes with shaved ice.

There was a comic book store next to May's, where comics with the covers torn off sold for five cents each. I was afraid of the old man who ran the place, and would make my mother come inside with me while I picked through the bushel baskets full of comics, looking for the ones I wanted. The old man never greeted us. He sat on a stool up front, with his elbows on the counter, grumbling and running his spotted hands through his yellowing white hair. When I took the comics I had chosen to the front, he would quickly count them, take my money, and hand back any change, all without a word. He seemed to be as eager to get rid of me as I was to be gone.

"Goddamn snakes," I heard him say one day. I looked up to see who he was talking to, but no one else was there. He was sitting at the counter, pulling at his hair as if there were some pain inside his head that he was trying to get hold of. He didn't see me looking at him.

•

HARLAN AND I WERE elaborately polite with each other, as if we were strangers who had moved by accident into the same house and spoke only fragments of each other's language. We'd squeeze past each other in the hall, muttering, "excuse me," and at night, if I was in the bathroom too long, he would tap lightly on the door and clear his throat. It was rare for us to speak directly, beyond courtesies. He was taller than my father, with thick, roughened hands and knobby wrists. I had noticed how he'd stand when he was talking to another person—with his weight on one foot and his other hip thrown out to the side—and I realized he did this in order to seem shorter.

"Harlan isn't used to being around children," Mother said. "But he'll get used to it. You'll see."

•

MY FATHER HAD MOVED into a new apartment complex, where there was a clubhouse and a swimming pool. His apartment had a small back patio; the first night I was there we grilled steaks and baked potatoes on the barbecue.

"Tomorrow," he said, "I thought we might get kites. We could take a picnic lunch out to a park and fly kites. How's that sound?"

"That sounds good," I said.

"We could ask Dana if she wants to come along," he said. "But only if you want to meet her. This is your weekend. We'll play it any way you want."

"Sure," I said. "She can come."

He had started telling me about Dana at the bus station, before we'd even made it to the car. He said they'd been dating six months and that she had made him take a hard look at his own life. "I was to the point," he said, "where I just didn't give a shit. I really didn't. Dana changed all that."

He also told me that he had a new job, keeping books at a meat packing plant. That's where he'd met Dana; she was the boss's secretary.

·

THE NEXT DAY DANA came over, and we got picnic stuff and kites and took them to a nearby schoolyard. She wasn't what I had expected: I thought my father would have some kind of bombshell girlfriend, but Dana was skinny and had a face like a rabbit—big front teeth and little eyes, set wide apart. Her fingernails were chewed down to the nub, and her fingertips were stained from all the Kools she smoked. She had beautiful red hair, but that was about the best that could be said for her. I thought she was plain old homely.

She called my father "sweetie," and tousled his hair with her fingers while he drove. When we'd parked in the school's parking lot, she said, "No, sweetie. Over there," and made him move the car so we would be five yards closer to a picnic table.

After we'd unpacked the car, she had me hold her kite while she played out the string for twenty yards or so, and when she told me to, I let go, and she took off running. My father and I whooped when the kite shot straight up in the air. Dana turned around and let the string run off the spool until the kite was way up. She knew how to make it dip and dive, and when she'd helped me get my kite up, she showed me how to maneuver it, and then we had a mock fight, each of us making feints and lunges at the other's kite. Every time we came close to colliding, she'd shout, "Hold on, Harold!" and let out a squawking, surprised laugh.

"I have three brothers," she told me. "That's how I know this stuff."

She had me take her kite while she ran over to the picnic table to get another cigarette, and when she came back, she said, "Your dad says come on and eat a bite, but I told him we're not ready. Unless you feel like pulling the kites in?"

"No," I said. "Not yet."

"All right, then. He can just cool his heels."

That night we grilled more steaks, and we made peppermint ice cream in an ice cream freezer Dana brought over. Later we put on our suits and played Marco Polo in the pool.

"I'll let you in on a little secret," Dana said to me, while we waited by the pool for Dad to bring towels out for us. "But you can't tell."

"Sure," I said.

"Your dad's about to get a big promotion. He doesn't know it yet, but he's going to be making a lot more than he makes now."

Dad was on his way across the pool deck with the stack of towels, and so I nodded, not wanting to say anything that he might overhear. Dana leaned closer to me. "You should be very proud of him," she whispered.

•

SUNDAY AFTERNOON DAD DROVE me to the Continental Trailways station. We got there early, bought my ticket, and went back to his car to wait.

"I have done one piss poor job," he said, "as far as being a good dad. But I promise things are going to be different from now on."

We sat in silence for a minute, and then he said, "I know your birthday's coming up, and I was wondering if there's something special that you'd like to have."

"A telescope," I said. I had found a book about astronomy mixed in with the comics at the comic book store, and had flipped through the pictures before putting it back. The idea about the telescope had just formed in the instant.

"Okay," he said. "All right. A telescope it is."

When it was time to go, he walked me across the street and hugged me before I got onto the bus. He smelled like the hairspray Dana had got him started using on his hair. "Next weekend you're up, we'll go see the motorcycle races," he said. "Dana's brother races a Ducati."

•

WHEN THE HOUSE WAS cleaned up and refurbished and all our belongings were unpacked and put away, Mother went out to buy some new things. First thing, she had wall-to-wall shag carpeting put in. Then she bought new appliances, all of them a color she called "avocado green"; the refrigerator had an ice maker that made ice shaped like half-moons. She bought me a French Provincial bedroom suite, which was more to her taste than mine, and, as an early birthday present, a small color television set.

"You need an air conditioner in your room more than you need a TV set," she said. "But that will have to wait. I knew you'd rather have the TV."

For the living room she bought a new couch, a recliner, and an armchair, all upholstered in crushed velvet, and a walnut console stereo with an AM/FM tuner and a turntable.

Harlan showed no sign that he begrudged the money she was spending, or that he felt strapped. He took off his boots and socks and walked around in bare feet on the new shag carpet and admired it. He sat on the new couch, and the new armchair, put his feet up in the new recliner, and said that it was heaven on a stick.

But a few years later, Harlan would chop that stereo to pieces with an axe, right there in the living room, and when he finished, he would break my mother's records, one by one, in pieces, and throw the pieces into the fireplace. She had Sam Cooke records, Ray Charles, Joan Baez, and Barbra Streisand. He would say he never wanted to hear a piece of music by a nigger, or a nigger-lover, or a Jew in his house again.

•

A PACKAGE ARRIVED ON my birthday, but it wasn't from my dad. The address was written out in blue ink, in a trembling, old-fashioned hand. I tore off the paper—brown bags from the grocery store—and inside the box I found a Quaker Oatmeal carton filled with marbles, the locomotive from an electric train set, and three silver dollars. I poured the marbles out onto the carpet and looked through them. I could tell that they were old: glass tiger's eyes, steelies, blue and white milk glass, several chalkies. There were seven or eight larger marbles, shooters, mixed in with the others.

The card inside was meant for someone younger than I, with its drawing of a small boy in a fire engine, a Dalmatian sitting on the seat beside him. It looked as if it had been saved in someone's dresser drawer for years; the edges had frayed and were starting to turn brown. Inside it said, simply, Happy Birthday. It was signed by Mrs. Frame.

Later that afternoon Mother and I went to the drive-in for banana splits, and then we went into the comic book store. The old man was there, as usual, behind the counter, grumbling and combing his hair with his fingers. Mother looked through old copies of *Life* magazine while I went through the baskets.

The book I was looking for was still there—the one about astronomy. I brushed the dust off of it and took it to the front.

"How much for this one?" I asked.

The old man picked the book up, turned it over, and then set it back down on the counter. "Take it," he said.

I just looked at him.

"It's your birthday, isn't it?" he said.

I nodded.

Back in the car, I asked my mother, "Did you tell him it's my birthday?"

"No," she said, "I didn't. I have no idea how he knew."

•

THAT NIGHT MOTHER ASKED me to show Harlan the presents Mrs. Frame had sent me. I brought them to the kitchen table. He took the top off the oatmeal box and scooped some marbles out with his hand.

"These were mine," he said, "when I was your age. The train, too. I don't know what happened to the rest of it, but my parents gave me that train for a Christmas present. That was just about the best surprise I ever had."

I hesitated for a moment, then I said, "They're yours, then. You should keep them."

He shook his head and poured the marbles back into the box. "No," he said, "they're yours now. Someday you might want to give them to your son."

Harlan said he had a present for me, too, but I would have to wait to get it. He said he would let me know when it was ready.

Before I went to bed that night, I tried to call my dad, but the telephone just rang and rang, and no one answered.

•

I SPENT HOURS STUDYING the pictures and descriptions in that book. There were color plates of galaxies and nebulae and planets. I had never seen a picture of the Horsehead Nebula, in

Orion, or the Veil Nebula, with its pink and blue glow. The Milky Way, the book said, was made up of a hundred thousand million stars; the red spot on the planet Jupiter was actually a storm that had been raging, now, for several hundred years; the craters on the moon were astroblemes, a word that means "star wounds."

At night I went into the back yard, watched for shooting stars, and picked out planets and the constellations. Mars was red; Venus bluish white. I thought about the light that had left those stars a million years or more before, and was just now reaching my eyes. I was looking at a picture of the way the stars were, way back then, and not how they were now. The sky we saw was an illusion, everything had long since changed, but we went right on believing we were seeing things as they are.

•

THE WEEK AFTER MY birthday I got a postcard from my dad. It was a photograph of him and Dana that they'd had taken in Las Vegas. They were standing, arm in arm, in front of a horseshoe-shaped display case that contained a million dollars. Dad looked groggy and disheveled; at his side a bottle of beer dangled from his hand. Dana's smile was tense and grudging, as if she'd been forced to pose. She gripped my father's elbow with both hands and looked directly at the camera, her small eyes narrowed in anticipation of the flash.

"We decided to come out to Vegas to get hitched," the postcard said. "Which looks better, do you think—your new stepmom, or that million bucks? Ha! Will call when we get back to Amarillo. Love you, Dad."

•

HARLAN CAME INTO MY room one morning that same week

and shook me by the shoulder. "Get up," he said, "I want to show you something."

I got out of bed, put on my clothes, and went into the living room. Harlan was standing by the front door with his hat on. "Come on," he said.

The sun was not yet over the horizon, and the sky was just beginning to turn light. But when I looked into the sky, I saw a shooting star, and then two more. Then I saw three and four at one time, some no more than a brief flash, others a long streak across the sky. I thought, at first, that this was what Harlan had brought me outside to see, but he had already climbed into his truck.

We drove south, and as we drove I rolled the window down and put my head outside to watch the shower of stars.

"They were saying on the news last night that this was starting," Harlan said. "They said it was a once-a-year deal. The Perseds."

I brought my head back inside. "*Perseids*," I said. "They're named for one of those Greek gods."

Harlan leaned over the wheel to get a better look. "It's something, all right," he said. "Never seen so many at one time."

The meteors, I knew, were chunks of rock, debris, that orbited the sun and burned up in our atmosphere when their orbits intersected ours.

We pulled off the road eventually, went through a gate, and drove across a rutted pasture towards a rusting tractor shed. Harlan's cows were huddled there, waiting for the sun to warm them before they wandered off to graze. There were eight or nine cows, Herefords, and one Angus bull. As the truck approached, the cows jostled one another nervously, and I saw a tiny black and white calf, suckling.

Harlan let the truck roll to a stop and then shut off the engine.

I wasn't sure why Harlan had brought me out there. He saw my confusion and said, "That bull calf is your birthday present. Remember I told you that you'd have to wait until it was ready?"

"Thank you," I said. "Thanks."

Harlan put his head out the window and yelled, "*Sooo-eee!*" The cows began to walk towards us.

"I thought it would be good for you," he said, "to raise something as your own."

We sat there and watched the cows. They looked at us with big, wet eyes, dreamy and expectant, as if they'd been promised something for their trouble. The small calf shivered by its mother's side.

Then we headed back to town. I looked out the window at the fence posts whipping by along the roadside, the long, green rows of cotton stretching to the far horizon. Meteors etched white lines in the milk-glass sky. Harlan spoke, but I did not hear what he said. I put my head outside and turned my face into the wind. It made my eyes tear, and I had to close them. An alphabet of lights flared in the dark behind my eyelids, and then faded, and my head filled with the empty, rushing noise. I stayed like that the rest of the way home.

The Drowned

FARDIN'S MORTUARY WAS SITUATED at the end of *Rue de l'Enterrement*, on one corner of the T where the street ran into *Boulevard Dehoux*. The building wasn't much: two stories of adobe stuck together, Lyle supposed, to fit the lot, its corners met as if by accident. Some iron grillwork on the second floor hung loose above a window, like a false eyelash come unglued.

Lyle brushed the fine white powder off the shoulder of his jacket. His car's air conditioner had gone out, so for a week he'd driven with the windows open, breathing in the dust and taxi fumes. He'd gone back to smoking. There didn't seem to be much point, just now, in quitting.

Before he rolled the window up, he smoked the last cigarette in the pack. Then he sat a moment, going over what he had to say. Half a block away an army transport exited the *caserne Dessalines* and turned in Lyle's direction. The *caserne* was a prison and an army barracks. Years before, he had been told, the enemies of Papa Doc were tortured there. Lyle watched the empty transport pass, listened to the sound of loose chains rattling against its sides. He waited to get out until the sound receded into traffic and the dust had cleared.

•

THE MORTUARY'S OFFICE SMELLED of ink and sulfur matches. Already Lyle felt queasy from the odor and the heat; he hoped he wouldn't be kept waiting. A small electric fan hummed, uselessly, in one corner of the room, and from the wall above the wooden desk a grinning Papa Doc surveyed the tiny room. The man had been dead ten years, but that photo hung on walls all over Port-au-Prince. In certain other business establishments one might also see a picture of the Pope. Lyle sat on a folding chair and felt a drop of sweat run down his calf.

Monsieur Fardin came through the door a moment later—a short, stout man in a vest and tie who had the white sleeves of his shirt rolled back and was wiping his hands on a towel.

"Excuse the hands," he said, setting the towel on the desk and turning up his clean, pink palms for Lyle to see. "I've been changing oil."

Lyle stood, and now, not knowing what to do with his own hands, held them out, palms up. Both men laughed.

"Sit down," Fardin said, and went around the desk. "You're from the embassy."

"The U.S. embassy," Lyle said.

"What other?" Fardin smiled. He sat. "How can I help you?"

"I've come about the drowning victims."

Fardin brought his hands together on his desk. "The bodies are upstairs. But I must apologize. They were delivered only yesterday, and so not all of them have been prepared. There are twenty-three."

A week had passed now since the bodies had washed up on a beach in Ft. Myers, Florida. The wooden fishing vessel that had carried them across the ocean, then the Gulf, had capsized in the surf and all but two had drowned. Economic refugees, the State Department said. These, like all the rest, were fleeing poverty, not persecution. And these, like all the rest, would be returned to Haïti.

"It's not the bodies, actually, I came to see about," Lyle said.

"Oh?"

"We've had calls about the coffins."

"Yes?"

"The bodies *are* in coffins?"

"Of course."

Lyle touched his temple with a handkerchief. "We've heard that wooden coffins have been substituted for the ones the U.S. government provided."

Fardin did not appear to be offended.

"Not at all," he said. "They are in the coffins they were shipped in."

"There was controversy, you know, in the States. Whether to return the bodies here for burial."

"A sad thing," Fardin said. "All those people, and so close to land."

"It's very sad, yes. And if the coffins were…" (What was the neutral word?) "…replaced…" He pulled his shoulders slightly up, as if his sentence was completed by the gesture. But Fardin pretended not to understand.

"It wouldn't look good if the coffins were replaced," Lyle said.

Fardin nodded.

"Have any of the families come?" Lyle asked. "To claim the remains?"

"Two or three. But all the victims were from the north of Haïti, quite far from Port-au-Prince. It would be impractical to take a body such a distance on those roads. And, as you know, the President-for-Life has donated crypts in the municipal cemetery."

"So I heard." Lyle waited, thinking Fardin might go on, but the man just sat there with a patient smile. Lyle looked around the room, uneasily, hoping to find something to admire, but his eye went once again to the photograph of Papa Doc. He stood and extended his hand. "I needn't go upstairs, I think. I'm sorry to have troubled you."

Fardin took his hand and bowed.

•

LYLE LOOKED FORWARD TO his mid-day meal. The quiet hour that he spent at home, away from all the hurry and confusion of the embassy, was worth the trouble of the drive. In the dining room, alone, absurdly, at a table that sat twelve, he'd clear his mind of all the nagging, petty details of his work.

It surprised him how his job seemed, more and more, a thing from which he had to have relief. He'd never felt used up like this at other posts. He'd mentioned his fatigue to Dr. Alvarez, but Alvarez had only said he needed leave.

Rose was working in the kitchen, her radio—as always—turned to news. The broadcast was in Creole, but the words "Ft. Myers" caught his ear at intervals. He knew that they were talking of the drownings. He set his wine glass down and bent his head, attempting to regain his ignorance. It was no use. He turned his head and called into the kitchen, "Rose!" Immediately the radio went silent and in its place he heard the sound her sandals made against the tiled floor.

"*Messer* Lyle?"

He regretted his impatience. "I've had enough to eat, Rose, thank you. It was very good."

She moved around the table, silently, collecting dishes on a tray. Her thin arms might have been a child's, and he felt, once again, the pity he had felt for her that afternoon when Alvarez had brought him to her on the wharf. It was a kind of reassurance, to feel compassion for another person. She would never understand that he was grateful to her for it.

"Rose?"

She looked at him, as if expecting to receive a reprimand, and the look undid his intention to say he wasn't angry at her. She'd seemed easily upset these past few days; he wondered, briefly, why. He made a helpless gesture with his hands. "I'm sorry," he said. "I've forgotten what I meant to say."

•

HE WENT ONTO THE terrace to have a cigarette, but when he touched the pocket of his jacket he remembered he'd run out. He slipped his wristwatch off and put it in his pocket, to remind him later to buy more. It was past time for him to leave, but he could not deny himself ten minutes in the fresher, hillside air. Why did the distances appear so vast? The ships docked at the wharf were toys; to reach them might have taken days instead of minutes. He knew better than to trust appearances, but he was tired of knowing that. He couldn't see what good it did, always knowing there was less to everything than met the eye.

"*Messer* Lyle?"

He turned and saw Rose standing in the doorway, clutching her apron.

"Yes, Rose?"

"In the morning, I will go to the doctor."

"Have you not been feeling well? You're taking all your pills, I hope."

"For an examination; the doctor wants to listen to the heart."

"What time is your appointment? I won't be free to take you in the morning, but I can send a driver."

"No. It's only that I want to tell you that I won't be here to serve the lunch. I'll put it in the cold box. The doctor says it's good for me to walk."

"All right. But don't make lunch. I won't have time to come back here tomorrow."

Driving to the embassy, he worried over her appointment. Her heart was weakened from some childhood fever, and the strain of being in the boat had nearly killed her. Dr. Alvarez had told him that she'd never be entirely well. "Her heart could fail at any time, for any reason," he'd said. "She might also live as long a life as you or me."

Lyle remembered asking if the heart could be repaired through surgery, and Alvarez's curt reply: "Perhaps. At great expense." He seemed to believe the matter ended there. Lyle feared to let himself think otherwise; better not to have illusions.

•

ART FRELENG NEVER LOOKED entirely comfortable behind his desk. A nervous man who chewed a pipe but never smoked it, he was married to a woman who, reportedly, had carried on affairs in every foreign post and Washington. People liked to say this was the reason he would never make ambassador, but Lyle thought otherwise. Art fit the role of DCM too well: a worrier, obsessed with detail, more comfortable with paperwork than people. He preferred to work behind the scenes, the perfect second-in-command.

Five years earlier, perhaps, Lyle would have gone along with this idea that Art had failed to live up to his promise, that he was a man who'd passed the point in life where he could reasonably hope for more. Somewhere in those years, Lyle realized, he'd passed that point himself. He'd served in the Foreign Service fifteen years, in seven countries. He could put in five more years and then retire. That was his ambition now: a pension, not to have to work. Art had, in fact, achieved a higher grade than Lyle could hope for now. Lyle envied him.

"You think Fardin was lying?" Art asked.

"He was evasive, but he might have thought I wanted to inspect the corpses—they're probably a mess. He struck me as a man who takes a certain pride in his profession."

"I wish you'd gone ahead and looked at them—the caskets, that is."

"I thought I'd better not. If he's taken them already, he has time to put them back. I didn't want to catch him lying. He could only go against us then, to save his pride."

"Last thing we need is those caskets showing up for sale somewhere in town." Art tugged a loose thread on his shirt cuff. "You weren't here, the last time something like that happened. It embarrassed us."

Lyle waited, with his hands locked in his lap, for Art to let him get back to his work. A moment passed in which Art seemed to be considering. "All right," he said. "All right. You're going to the funeral tomorrow?"

"I'd planned to, yes."

"That's fine. Before you go, you'd better have a look at this."

Art pulled a sheet of paper from the combination file behind his desk and handed it to Lyle. The paper had a different quality, a different feel, than what Department cables came on; the text was blue, instead of black, and single-spaced, which made it difficult to read. It was the way the Agency did everything—even cables were a kind of hostile action. In the middle of the page three names appeared. One of them was circled.

"Quite a shock," Art said when Lyle looked up. "I find it hard to believe myself."

Lyle read the cable through again. The circled name was that of Dr. Juan Emilio de Santillana Alvarez, and further down he was described: a Cuban émigré who'd settled first in the Dominican Republic, then in Haïti, after Castro came to power. His patients in Port-au-Prince had, for years, included diplomats from western embassies, including the United States. Alvarez, the cable said, was working—had been working—for some indefinite period of time—as an agent of the Cuban government.

Lyle laid the cable on the desk. "Don't believe it, then. I don't. What do they mean by 'agent' anyway? That's awfully vague."

"You know what 'agent' means as well as I."

"And *you* know Alvarez."

Art sighed. "I thought I did." He pushed back from his desk and reached into a drawer. Lyle waited for him to present proof: an envelope of photographs, an intercept.

But he wouldn't need to look at it to know. He knew already. Despite himself he believed the accusation, and he believed so easily because it didn't contradict who Alvarez was. It was something more to know, not something different: an uncomfortable truth, but not a damning one. Cuba was an adversary nation, Haïti a friend. That was policy, and Lyle was obligated to support it by his words and actions. But his feelings were his own. If Alvarez was working for his native country, it was no different than what Lyle himself did.

Art found what he was looking for and shut the drawer. He held his pipe up, rubbed its bone-smooth bowl.

"I hope they're certain," Lyle said.

"I think they must be."

"Do the Haïtians know?"

"They may suspect, although we haven't told them anything. The Europeans and Canadians will be informed this afternoon. I'll be more than sorry if he's caught—but of course it's none of our affair. We can't interfere."

"I suppose not."

"Well, I wanted you to be aware. You used Alvarez, I know. We all did. Now we'll have to use the embassy's man in the DR or the Navy doctor at Guantanamo. Don't think I've ever seen the Navy man without a razor cut. Doesn't put your mind at ease."

"Won't it look suspicious, if Alvarez's embassy patients drop him all at once?"

"Maybe. But we can't risk further contact. Anyway, I'd be surprised if he's around much longer."

Lyle took that in; what, exactly, did it *mean*?

"I only mean I wouldn't be surprised if he's tipped off by someone at the other embassies. He has a lot of friends."

Lyle stood. He pulled the creases of his pants legs, absently, until he got them straight. "Grateful patients, too. I wouldn't want to be the one to turn him over to this government."

"Nor I," said Art.

•

THE RAIN CAME SHORTLY after dinner. Lyle sat in his den, a novel in his lap, and waited for the moment when the power would go out. In the evening, if the lights stayed on, he liked to read. When the lights went out they stayed out hours. There was nothing for it, nothing left to do but listen to the battery-run radio, and broadcasts drifted in a storm.

Tonight it didn't matter. The novel irritated him. A poorly-written thriller—with betrayals and state secrets and the safety of the free world riding on a single man—it struck him as more ludicrous than most. How much could one man do?

He was thinking of the wharf, the afternoon the U.S. Coast Guard cutter brought the people in from Rose's boat. He'd kept his eye on Alvarez among them, joking, sympathizing, using his doctor's authority to shield them, for a time, from the Haïtian military officers who stood waiting to record their names. Lyle had been surprised when Alvarez came over to him.

"You're looking still for someone to clean house and cook?" he'd asked, and Lyle, not knowing what he had in mind, said yes. Alvarez then brought him over to meet Rose. "This one speaks a little French," he said. "She says that she can cook. She has no family. There's nowhere for her to go back to."

Lyle set down the book and went into the dining room. He poured himself a half a glass of bourbon, then reconsidered and poured until the glass was almost filled. Before he put the cap back on he took a shot directly from the bottle, swished it in his mouth, like Listerine. He shuddered when he swallowed.

Through the open door onto the terrace he could see the dark trees shaking in the wind. Lightning struck close by, and in its flash he saw the pink hibiscus in the cachepot, riotous with blooms. The lights dimmed, then went out.

He set the glass down and went to find a candle in the kitchen drawer. The twilight was enough to see by, but the room was filled with shadows, and he didn't see Rose until she came between him and the window. He'd thought she had already gone downstairs, to her apartment.

"You'll need candles if you haven't got some," he said, searching for the box. He found it, took a candle out and held it to a burner of the stove. He turned the knob, and watched the ring of blue gas flower in the dark. He dripped wax in an ashtray then set the candle in the wax. When he'd done the same thing with another, he turned to offer one to Rose.

She didn't take it, and when he held it closer to her he saw her shiver. Never had she seemed to him so much a child; not even on the wharf that afternoon when she had looked at him in just this way, expecting nothing. Never had he seen despair, such hopelessness, so closely. It had been his impulse, then, to save her, as it was his impulse now to take her to him. But he told himself, *She's not a child*. He set the ashtray on the countertop, between them, and the candle's yellow light fell on her dress.

"What is it, Rose? The storm can't hurt you."

She stood where she was, not answering, until he began to fear she must be ill. The light had gone completely now; the rain came down. The roads would flood; he wasn't sure that he could get her to the doctor if he had to. Then, he realized, he wouldn't know where else to take her, if he couldn't go to Alvarez. He took her arm and led her to the kitchen table.

He sat with her, wondering whether he should try the phone, when she spoke in a whisper.

"I'm afraid."

"It's only thunder."

"Not the storm."

"What, then?"

She ran her hand along her forearm, as if trying to keep warm, and looked away. "I am afraid to die," she said.

"You won't die, Rose."

They sat in silence, watching as the candles burned, listening to the gusts of rain against the house. At last, she said that she was tired, and thought that she should sleep now, but she shivered once again and he got up to get a sweater for her from his bedroom. On his dresser, where he'd laid his wallet and his keys, there was a pad of paper and a pen. As if he'd planned to do exactly this, he wrote two words—*They know*—and put the paper in his pocket.

The house was built into a hill, and Rose's room was on the bottom level. Lyle had not been in here since the first day he had brought her to the house, and helped her bring the necessary furniture downstairs. He swept his flashlight beam around the neat, bare room which looked exactly as it had that first day, but for pictures on the wall that she had taken from a calendar he'd given her. A mountain range in Colorado. Autumn in New England. Surf off Monterey.

"You'll be all right," he said, waiting as she set the lighted candle on the table, and lit another on the stand beside her bed. She said "yes," and thanked him. Still he stood there, thinking nothing for the time, until he realized that she was watching him. He pulled the note from his pocket and held it out to her.

"Give this to Dr. Alvarez tomorrow. Tell him it's from me."

She took the paper, and he said good night. He started out, then came back.

"The paper has to go to Alvarez. Remember that. You mustn't give it to his nurse or anybody else. Only Alvarez."

She said she understood.

He went outside and ran across the courtyard, through the chilling rain, and up the stairs.

•

Across the street from the main entrance to the *caserne Dessalines* there was a store where Lyle knew he could buy cigarettes. He'd forgotten to buy a pack the day before, and knew he'd need another to get by until the commissary opened later in the afternoon.

While he waited for a girl to change his ten-*gourde* note he watched the gate across the street. Young soldiers stood inside the gate, leaning lazily against their ancient Mausers. The oldest one of them, Lyle thought, is younger than his rifle. They seemed to have no interest in the crowd that moved along the street in the direction of the cemetery and Fardin's. A jeep pulled up, and a soldier swung the gate in so that it could enter. Before he closed the gate again someone shouted and he held it open. A moment later a woman came out of the courtyard into the street. She was thirty yards from where Lyle stood, and he couldn't see her face. But he recognized the pattern on the fabric of her housedress, and the way the woman kept her head down as she walked reminded him of Rose. He was almost certain it *was* Rose.

He tried to follow, but rain the night before had turned the streets to mud, and he had trouble catching up to her. The crowd was gathered at the corner, at the Mortuary, and when he couldn't get through, he gave up. There might have been five hundred people there. He couldn't hope to find her in a crowd that size.

He opened the new pack, removed a cigarette and lit it with a match. He was worried. If it was Rose he'd seen... Well, what of it? Alvarez's office was no more than a few blocks from the spot. But why would Rose have gone inside the *caserne*? If she had a friend or relative in prison, she'd have told him. As far as he knew she had no one.

Were the Haïtians trying to get information from her about him?

She'd be vulnerable to pressure. They'd consider her an undesirable—disloyal because she'd tried to leave the island. She could be jailed, and there'd be nothing he could do to help her. But she had no information she could share with them. Not that they could use. But there was something else, now, she could give them.

He dropped the cigarette, half-finished, in the mud, and turned back through the crowd. When he got free of them he took his jacket off and carried it. The sun had risen high into a cloudless sky, and the beginning of the day's heat lifted from the muck a faint, unpleasant odor of decay. Five minutes later, his shirt soaked through, Lyle was at the door of Alvarez's office. It was locked. A note taped to the door's glass explained the office would be closed until the afternoon, in order that the doctor might attend a funeral.

By the time Lyle returned, people were moving from Fardin's to the cemetery. Fardin's men were carrying the caskets down the stairs, and loading them in hearses. The caskets were identical: a soldier's silver-gray, official issue, Government of the United States.

Lyle stood nearby and watched the mourners leave the chapel. Alvarez was not among them.

•

THERE WERE TWICE AS many people in the cemetery as had been outside Fardin's. Here the ground was even softer, and debris the storm had washed down from the hills had not been cleared away. Lyle had to step around, or over, garbage on the paths. The sun reflecting off the whitewashed mausoleums was blinding. The place smelled foul.

It was impossible to avoid the muck. His shoes were covered with it, the bottoms of his trouser legs were spattered. Other people began to take their shoes and sandals off and carry them. Men were rolling up their pants cuffs.

Lyle edged between the mausoleums, but couldn't see the hearses, or the caskets, or the crypts where they were to be interred. He scanned the crowd for anyone with light skin, brown, like Alvarez's, caught up once to someone with the same build, called out, "Alvarez," but the man who stopped and turned around looked nothing like Alvarez.

He came to a place where everyone had stopped, were trying to see above the heads of those in front of them, and Lyle stopped, too. He couldn't think. The crowd pushed in against him. He heard men shouting in exasperated voices; a woman wailed, and cries and sobs broke out around him. Then, suddenly, the crowd grew quiet. Lyle put his hand above his eyes, to shade them, and tried to get the attention of a young man standing on the crypt above him.

"Please," he said, "what's happening?"

The man did not look down at him.

"Please," Lyle said. "I need to know. What's going on?"

The man replied in Creole. Lyle didn't understand exactly what he'd said, although he thought he'd heard the man say "hammer."

The man removed his torn straw hat and held it at his side. Lyle heard a loud, dull thud, the sound of metal hitting metal, then another, and the crowd began to wail again, more loudly than before.

"What is it," Lyle said. "What about the hammer?"

"The coffins," said the man. "They are too high."

He understood. The sound was hammering. The coffins were too high. They wouldn't fit into the crypts designed to hold pine boxes. Fardin's men were pounding down the lids to make them fit.

Lyle pushed through the suffocating crowd, trying to escape the crush, the smell of sweat. The sound of hammers echoed off the mausoleums like bullets. Ahead, he saw Monsieur Fardin emerging from between two crypts. He ran to catch him.

"Yes," Fardin explained. "We had no choice. We had to use the hammers." He smiled complacently at Lyle. "I would never, as a man of business, think to do it. But *you*, Monsieur. *You* are the diplomat. No doubt you understand, more perfectly than I, the relevant political considerations."

Lyle returned, as stiffly as he could, the stiff bow Fardin offered him, then watched the man make his way, unhurried, toward the cemetery gate. A hearse was going out, but stopped and backed up to allow a jeep to come inside. The jeep sped by Lyle without slowing. One soldier drove, and another, in the back seat, held his Mauser so that it was pointed at the sky. An officer was in the front seat, opposite the driver.

Lyle made his way back to the same crypt, where the young man stood, still holding his ragged hat, still with his rapt expression. Lyle tried to pull himself up onto the crypt. The man looked down and waved him off.

"No room," he said. "No room."

"Let me up there," Lyle said. "Please." He held out the pack of cigarettes, the man accepted them, and offered Lyle his hand to help him up.

Now Lyle could see the caskets on the ground—all twenty-three of them, arranged in three neat rows. The men hammering the lids had taken off their shirts, and worked with fury as the crowd behind them wailed and shouted.

And, among them, Lyle saw Alvarez. The doctor had his glasses in one hand, and in the other was a clean, white handkerchief. Lyle watched the doctor polishing the lenses of his glasses, absorbed in this small task as though it were the most important thing he'd do that day.

When he dropped the handkerchief and bent to find it, Lyle began to shout his name. Alvarez stood up but gave no sign that he had heard.

Some little distance back, Lyle saw the barrel of the Mauser lifted high above the crowd, moving through it, seeking Alvarez, divining him.

In Print

WHEN I STOPPED TO pick up coffee at the Cubbyhole, all the little Asian ladies in there were talking excitedly about the earthquake. I thought it had just happened, while I was walking across campus from my car, and I was not surprised I hadn't felt a thing because I never do outside. But then I found out it had hit the night before, a 5.8 followed by two aftershocks. I'd slept right through them.

I thought of Annie right away. Everything reminded me of Annie then, because she'd just walked out on me two weeks before, but Annie's terrified of quakes and I thought I ought to call her just to see if she was all right.

But I knew her mother called her after every quake, to check on her, and I was only looking for another reason to try to talk to Annie.

And it isn't really accurate to say I slept right through them. I'd put half a fifth of bourbon down the night before, and several pain pills left from when my swimmer's shoulder got so bad. You aren't supposed to mix the pills with alcohol because you'll fall asleep, which was exactly what I wanted.

Normally I don't have pills around, or liquor either—I'd had to buy the Jack on my way home. But I had not been sleeping well since Annie left, and I'd decided it was time to try some numbing agents.

•

ANNIE LIVES A BLOCK off Haight Street in the City, on the top floor of an old Victorian that sways whenever there's a temblor. A few times I was with her there, at night, when one hit, and we'd roll against each other and hug tight, wondering if this would be The Big One. Which is exactly the wrong thing to do. You're supposed to get into a doorframe, or under sturdy furniture. But Annie never held me quite so tightly any other time and, after everything stopped jiggling, I'd thank God she lived in San Francisco.

Annie's from around here. Her mother lives on the Peninsula which means they both feel anything above a 4.0.

Oh, Annie. I hope Watney Fromm holds onto you in bed that way. I heard there was a quake once while a party was in progress, and Watney shoved Grace Paley out of a doorframe she just happened to be standing in. But I don't know. Maybe Watney is a better man than that and he just panicked. You hear things about Watney.

We're all writers. You've heard of Watney Fromm because his book of stories, "Material Illusions," was a *New York Times* bestseller, and he's only twenty-six. And you might have heard of Annie Campbell's novel, "Traces," which came out two years ago, and has that awful abstract drawing on the cover of the paperback. I told Annie once it looks like barbed wire wrapped around a baked potato, and she laughed but later told me that it pissed her off. You've never heard of me, unless you've seen the latest *Poison Toad*, or *Ziggurat*. Nathan Bang. That's my name, not another magazine. The names of magazines are in italics, because of Annie. I always thought they went in quotes, but Annie said that periodicals go in italics.

I write. My stories are in print. And last month I got twenty-seven hundred dollars from some lunatic foundation in Missoula "to improve your literary skill and talent." Annie called from New York on the day I got that letter, and I asked her if she thought the lunatic foundation gives money to writers they don't think need improving. And why twenty-seven hundred? Annie said that it was wonderful, and I was being negative as usual. She sounded proud of me, and I was happy I'd done something she was proud of. I didn't know that I'd already lost her.

•

WHAT HAPPENED IS THAT Annie came back from New York, where some British magazine had flown her for an interview (Can't they use the phone? I asked when Annie said she had a free trip), and she told me she'd met someone else.

In five days? I said. Five days and you're with another man? Let's work it out, I said. I love you. I'm confused, she said. She said she thought she was in love with this guy, that he might come west to see her in September, and if he wanted to she'd let him.

"I can't be with you, Nate," she said, "knowing you'd be hurt by that." And though I was determined not to beg, I begged, and then she made her exit from my sad, single-occupancy studio in Menlo Park, and from my newly miserable life.

Annie has the usual variety of writers' maladies, and then some. She writes first drafts in longhand and has to have this kind of pen, that kind of paper. She keeps a little one-cup hot plate on her desk to keep her Orange Zinger warm, and if—as sometimes happens—it gets cold anyway, it throws her whole day off.

We all have insecurities, anxieties, depression. I tell myself these are inevitable when what you do can be compared directly to the output of the greatest literary minds in history. I suppose it's like a baseball player always falling short of Babe Ruth's records, or Ty Cobb's. The difference is you can't put Ty Cobb and the latest phenom on the field to see just how they really do compare. Try reading out a page of

Madame Bovary, then reading what you've come up with that morning, or even what you've written, and re-written for the past six months. Annie's always pegging other writers—who's better than whom, who reviewed whose book, who's serious, who's not. I understand it, though I always thought it cost her more than it was worth.

•

It was a Monday night she left me. That week I wrote three short stories, put them in manila envelopes and sent them out. Normally it takes more time than that. But I couldn't bear to let my mind rest. I was writing like I had the devil at my heels, and I suppose I did. By Friday afternoon, though, I was bushed, and I could feel the devil closing in. I decided I'd go see Susan in the City.

Susan's not a writer; she's a graphic artist I met on a temp job in the days when I did word processing to pay the rent.

I introduced myself to Susan after I overheard her tell another temp, "Sometimes it is *such* a burden being psychic."

I think of Susan as my analyst. She nods and listens, stirs the ice cubes in her orange juice at eighteen rpm, and pouts sympathetically at appropriate moments. Susan resists drama, and I hoped her calmness might rub off on me.

It's good to tell your troubles to a friend who's not a writer. The thing about having writers for friends is that, inevitably, you talk about your problems. Then, six months later, you're thumbing through the latest *Severed Digit*, and in that issue there's a story by your friend and in the story there's a character who has *your* initials and *your* fucked-up life. The weird thing is you never feel exposed. You only think: You *bastard*. That was *my* material. *I* was going to use it.

•

I drove up to the City around 3:00 p.m., right when I

finished swimming, because I didn't want to hit the Friday evening rush on 101. And since I hadn't been in the City since before Annie went back east, I gravitated to the Haight, where I intended to hang out until five o'clock when Susan got off work. I hadn't eaten lunch, and I had only just sat down in Zona Rosa with a chicken taco when I looked up through the window and saw Annie walking towards me hand-in-hand with Mr. Marvelous. He had fair skin, light brown hair, arms and shoulders that were like what God's blueprint for arms and shoulders must have been. I could swim the English Channel twice a day and never match those shoulders. I could see all this because he had a tank-top on. Of course I tossed my taco.

It raised questions. Was this the guy from New York, come to visit six weeks early, or some other guy? And if it was some other guy, had they been together all along? And since this guy looked like a model, could he be smart, too? That bite of taco was the last meal I would have for days.

I waited for what seemed a decent interval, then left to go directly to my car. Half a block up Haight, though, I saw Annie and her friend. They'd turned around and were heading towards me. This time Annie saw me, too, although I'd seen them first and had time enough to look as if I hadn't. There was nowhere I could duck, but as it turned out Annie did the ducking. She grabbed Watney by the hand and dragged him through traffic to the other side of Haight.

I didn't know that it was Watney then. I knew Watney was her next-door neighbor, that they'd both been undergrads at Stanford, and that she thought his work was "thin." But I had never met him. One time we were going into Annie's and he was backing his black Porsche out of the garage next door. "That's Watney," she said, but the Porsche had tinted windows and I couldn't see inside. Watney rolled his window down a wee bit, nodded at us like a movie star, then drove away. I didn't want to base my whole impression of the guy on that one moment.

Annie had told me that Watney was having a hard time with a novel he was trying to get started, and that they'd have coffee every now and then so she could tell him how she'd solved the problems she'd had writing hers. She told me that he had a girlfriend; for all I know, the girlfriend was in the Porsche with him that day. I never gave more thought to it than that. But seeing Annie pull the guy across the street put more questions in my head. She might have wanted to spare me the pain of running into them, but if it was the guy from back east then it wasn't like she'd kept him secret. I thought there had to be more going on.

·

ANNIE TEACHES AT SAN Francisco City College. I'm at Stanford University in Palo Alto. Annie taught here until last year and I've got her old job now. Watney doesn't have to work. I was a Stegner Fellow Annie's last year here, and then, the next year, Annie moved to City and I moved into Annie's old job. We'd been friendly with each other, but I'd never given Annie much thought because, although she's three years younger, she's a more established writer than I and I felt she wouldn't be interested in some guy who gets stories into *Bloated Lotus*. Then one night she called, said she was in P.A., and did I want to meet her for a drink at Antonio's Nut House? I had my guard up that night, for some reason, and I think she did, too, so we drank a few beers, said good night and nice to see you, and drove home in separate cars to separate beds. But I called her up that Saturday, stayed that night at her place in the Haight, and when a 4.7 hit I knew I was in love.

·

I HAVE AN OFFICE where I write. Obscure quarterlies seem to like it that I'm so prolific. I park my car out by the Stanford pool and hike the mile into the Quad. I get a large Vienna Roast at the Cubbyhole, and then I get to work: after opening my mail, chatting with the Program Secretary, and latching on to any other passers-through the nearly empty summer halls. That morning, after hearing about the earthquake I'd slept through, I went to my office and found a single piece of mail in my box: the *Department of English Newsletter*.

Of course I felt obliged to read it line by line, and I gave no more or less attention to the paragraph concerning Watney in the "News of Former Students" column than I did to any other newsy item. "Watney Fromm," it read, "B.A. '84, University of Iowa Writers Workshop '86, received the Louise Bedichek award for best short fiction of the year. Fromm's first book of stories, 'Material Illusions,' will appear in paperback this month."

The mind is an amazing thing. The subconscious, actually, as any writer can attest to. You're going along with What You Have In Mind; you have a plot, a character, you're smugly confident of How He's Going To Get What's Coming To Him, then, out of nowhere, there's a sentence on the page you didn't write. It just appeared. You may fight it for a good long while, but if you're any good at all you know that sentence is the only true thing in the story, and you have to throw away your comfortable plan and try to write the story that deserves that sentence. That's why writing's such a pain.

So I thought no more of Watney Fromm until that afternoon while I was swimming. People who've tried swimming and don't like it say it's boring. But I get a lot of writing done that way, and sometimes when I'm hard at something and

The Sentence still eludes me, the pool's the only place where I can coax it out of hiding. That day I kept losing count of laps, and my mind refused to fix on anything except the earthquake, and the fact that we were on alert, which meant that it was much more likely in the next few days that we would get The Big One.

What would happen if The Big One hit and I was in the middle of a lap? Would I and all that water drop into the open fissures of the earth, and could I swim within that perfect blue drop of a pool as I free-fell through all the planet's geologic strata? Or would the earth squeeze closed around me, spitting me into the buckled bleachers or the tossed and frothing hot tub by the diving well? Would I body surf to San Jose? And then, as I was coming home on the last 50 of a fast 200, I thought, "Watney Fromm."

·

WHEN I LEFT THE locker room I went directly to the campus bookstore. They had one copy of his hardback, and I pulled it off the shelf where Frisch and Gaddis held it up on either side. I opened to the back to check the jacket photograph, and there he was. Watney Fromm and Mr. Marvelous. Mr. Marvelous and Watney Fromm. The guy I'd tossed my taco for.

Sometimes I surprise myself. You'd think the news that Annie lied to me would make me go berserk. Confirming that I'd been thrown over for a younger, richer, more successful, and unquestionably striking man, should have made me miserable. But for the first time in two weeks I felt like my old self again. In fact, I laughed. I don't know why. Maybe from relief, because I'd been thinking that this guy would go back to New York, and when the next quake hit Annie was going to think of me, and maybe she'd come back. So I no longer had to live with that deluded hope. For another thing, the devil that you know is better than the devil that you don't. I had a rival, and I knew who he was. I was angry, but I felt okay.

•

LIKE I SAID, YOU hear things about Watney. Such as, his given name is John, but John Fromm sounds dull so he took his new name from a beer he likes because he thought it sounded literary. Like he was known in workshops for taking ideas from other peoples' stories—not turns of phrase or quirky gestures but plots, central incidents—and using them for his own. Like he had once said that his favorite writer is James Michener, and when he found out that wasn't cool he started saying Faulkner. This was a man who needed to be liked; I guess that's what a writer is.

•

I CALLED SUSAN FROM my office, because I thought she'd get a kick out of this new information, and she did, and although she's not a fiction reader she knew who Watney Fromm is from an article she'd read in *People* magazine, and that very day an ad had caught her eye as she was paging through the *Chron*—"Watney Fromm, author of [you know the title], will read and sign books, 8:00 p.m., at Words, Words, Words."

"He's quite the looker, isn't he," she said. "I saw his picture and I thought, He *can't* be *smart*."

She was telling me about her new boss, whom she hates, when I interrupted her.

"Will you go with me?"

"With you where?"

"Tonight. The reading."

"I can't imagine why you'd want to go."

I didn't know myself, to tell the truth, but a flash had gone off in my head, and an idea had formed from God knows what. As any writer knows, when something like that hits you, you do best to let it take you where it will.

•

I PICKED SUSAN UP at her apartment and drove like crazy through the early evening traffic of the City. I'd had time enough to pick up my address book, hit the bank on my way out of Palo Alto, and merge into the crawl of 101. To make things worse, there was a game at Candlestick that night, and so, until I got past Army Street, the traffic moved at twenty miles per hour.

"What's the hurry?" Susan asked, "It's just a little after seven now. The reading's not 'til eight."

"I know," I said, "We've got to get there early."

Parking is a problem in the City, but I found a spot on Market Street, two doors away from Words, Words, Words, and chose to take this as a sign that I was where I was supposed to be.

In the window of the bookstore was a nice big poster with that jacket photograph of Watney and the same announcement Susan had seen in the *Chron*, and when we went inside I saw a table stacked high with his paperbacks, and another propped up beside the register behind which sat a Bright Young Thing, flipping through *The Village Voice* in such a way as to let everybody know *she* knew *they* knew it was a once-hip has-been rag that could be mocked for its pretensions.

Watney was already there, with Annie. She was standing facing him in Self-Help, holding both his hands and talking to him in an earnest, fervent way I'd never seen in her. My heart dropped for an instant, seeing them, but I had known it would. They both looked over, and when Annie saw me she almost let go Watney's hands, but I smiled reassuringly in their direction and, for some unfathomable reason, flipped the peace sign at them.

Then I went directly to the register and took the paperback of Watney's book off its display stand.

"Is this good?" I asked The Bright Young Thing.

"*Very*," she said.

"Okay," I said. "I'll take your word for it. Give me twenty-seven hundred dollars' worth."

She must have used that same expression she gave me for all the kooks and hustlers who came in and tried to tell her about UFOs or the Great Unpublished Masterpiece that they had right there with them, in that greasy grocery sack beside their feet. That's the look she tried to use on me. But when I pulled the wad of money from my pocket and started laying hundred dollar bills on the counter, the corners of her mouth came up a bit, like she'd just burped.

"No need to count the books now," I said. "Just leave them where they are and don't let anybody move them. I'll want to have them signed."

•

I KNOW YOU'RE ASKING why I'd do this, and a writer hates to disappoint his readers, but the truth is, *I don't know.*

It makes no sense, not in any easy way, and maybe that's exactly *why* I did it. Maybe just because that's what a writer looks for: the unexpected gesture that reveals the character in some way that his explicable actions can't. It just seems right; it makes sense in that crazy, cantilevered logic that the world demands we use to get from one day to the next. It just seemed right, and so I did it. Somehow I was getting even, settling accounts. My twenty-seven hundred dollars, Watney's paperbacks. Maybe I just hoped to prove that when you try to figure out how much a book, a poem, a story's worth, you can't.

We all want money, and we all need praise and love, and if, one morning, we wake up to find the world's discovered us and wants to give us all those things, we may feel cheated and misunderstood. "It isn't me you want," we'll say. "It isn't me you love. It's just a book. You only love me for a lousy book."

Or maybe it's simpler than that. Maybe I was hoping Annie could accept the gesture and explain it better than I could myself. I hoped she might appreciate that I was trying to subvert the straight-on, worn-out sentiment of words, and tell her this way—this way that could make no sense—I loved her.

•

WATNEY READ. THERE WERE many people there, and many were disappointed that they couldn't buy a book. Afterwards I went up to the table, shook Watney's hand, and set the register receipt in front of him.

"I bought your book," I said.

He picked up the slip of paper, shook his head, and smiled at me.

"Thank you," he said.

"Would you sign them?"

"All of them?"

"I'd like that, if you would. Here's my address book. If you'd just go through it signing one for every person in there, then I have some more I'll tell you later."

Annie had come over, and they looked at one another, then at me; Watney rolled his right sleeve up and started signing.

"Could I talk to you a minute, Annie?" I asked.

•

WE WALKED TO THE back of the store and stood in Large Print, Annie leaning against the shelves and looking at the floor.

"Understand. I don't feel angry now," I said, controlling fury, "but I need to know one thing." She pursed her lips the way she does when she thinks someone's asking something of her that she doesn't want to give. "Just one thing, Annie. Why'd you lie to me? Did you think my fragile ego couldn't handle being dumped for someone younger, handsomer and richer than I? Why did you lie, Annie? Were you ashamed of *me*? Or of *him*?"

Now she looked at me. "I *never* was ashamed of you. You can't think that."

"I don't know what to think. You haven't given me enough to go on."

"I don't know, either, Nate. You were just too confident for me. You scared me that way. I kept trying to live up to what you are, how you are—your steadiness, your fuck-all attitude, the way you write only for yourself and no one else. I can't do that. I need the world to tell me I'm all right. And so does Watney. He's a mess. He needs me more than you."

Well, as I say, we're writers. We tell lies and call them stories, and we judge the quality of untruth with a practiced eye, and some appreciation, even while the lie is mangling our hearts.

"You don't know how wrong you are," I said. "I *always* needed you. I swear to God I'm just as big a mess as Watney. *Bigger*."

"No," she said, "You're not. You'll come through it all in one piece with another dozen stories to your credit. Watney can't write now, he can't do much of anything to make himself feel better. But he says I make him better, and I believe him."

"You're so wrong about me, Annie. But you're wrong about yourself, too. You don't need the world so much. I just wish you'd let me tell you that. I just wish you'd believe me."

I thought Annie was about to cry because she started trembling, but then an oversized biography fell off a shelf and almost hit her, and I pulled her toward me, held her head against my chest and bent my own above her while the lights flashed off and on and the floor rocked like a dory in a speed-boat's wake. More books tumbled off the shelves and landed at our feet.

It only lasted for a minute. And it was not The Big One, after all. But for the last time Annie held me like she used to, while we shook, and I leaned in and whispered in her ear, "We're going to be fine."

The Christmas Cathedral

IT TOOK THREE DAYS for Marcella Landers to feel guilty about her purchase, and then she thought herself guilty only of carelessness. She'd got a better bargain than even she, at first, imagined, but it had not been her intention to take advantage of the boy. That, certainly, would be less easy to excuse.

She hadn't made much effort to decorate for Christmas. No tree, of course. It was possible to buy them in the market at Kenscoff, but a small, lopsided pine went for fifteen or twenty dollars and it wasn't worth the trouble just for herself. She had set out two crèches: the white porcelain figures Phillip's mother found in Belgium, and the African-featured mahogany figures she had bought from a man in Pétion-Ville. The bookshelves and china cabinet displayed cards her friends had sent from the States or their foreign posts: Brazil, Honduras, Thailand, Finland, Romania. In the center of the dining room table she'd placed the cardboard-and-tissue-paper cathedral.

It was about twelve inches tall and eighteen inches long. The cardboard walls and steep roof fit together precisely, with no lumps of paste or ragged edges. The boy had cut four tall, gothic windows with pointed arches on each side and a rose window in front. Inside, for stained glass, he had pasted bits of colored tissue paper across the windows' small, irregular openings. In some places he overlapped blue and red for purple, or put a double layer to give a darker color or a layer of white and another color for a lighter shade. The front doors, a larger version of the arched windows, opened out from the middle on hinges of stiff fabric and fastened closed with a flat brass hook that looked to have come off a jewelry box. At night, when the two candles inside the cathedral were lighted, the windows sparkled like real stained glass. Marcella thought she had never seen anything so lovely.

She had paid a dollar for it.

That was Sunday night. Driving home from the Ambassador's reception, slightly drunk on red wine and filled a little with the Christmas spirit, she'd seen colored lights floating beside the road like fireflies and pulled her Plymouth onto the shoulder. Children surrounded the car, waving their lanterns. It was a custom in Haïti for children to make these Christmas lanterns, called *fanals*. Most were cathedrals or houses, but some of the children had made doves or partridges (she couldn't tell which), and she even saw one Christmas angel.

When she rolled down the window to speak to them she smelled sweat and something else: a sickroom smell that made her think of fever. Suddenly she was aware of her blouse clinging to her, and she reached up to pull the collar away from her throat. She wanted to get out of the car, where she would be cooler and could take a better look at the lanterns, but the children were too insistent, pressing up against the doors and windows and trying to get her attention with "*Madame! Madame!*" They were too many.

If she tried to get out they would be all over her. She saw a boy standing behind the crowd of children at her door, carefully steadying with one hand the cathedral he balanced on his head. She called him forward, hoping that by choosing the quiet boy she would show the others how proper behavior is rewarded.

He wanted three dollars, but that was just a bargaining

price. She never paid more than half the asking price, if that much.

"*Non.* One dollar," she said, holding up an index finger.

He looked pained, and asked for two. She repeated her gesture, and when he hesitated she turned away and put the car in gear. She pulled forward a few feet, and the boy yelled after her, "OK, Miss! OK! *Un dollar*, OK!" She stopped and reached over the seat to open the back door.

The boy set the *fanal* on the seat. When he leaned down to blow out the candles she saw, only for an instant, his face. His skin was dark and smooth, and fine gray dust from the road had settled around his eyes and in his hair. She turned the dome light on, took a single dollar bill from her purse and handed it to him through the window. He looked at it with no emotion, as if he had no idea what the bill had to do with him.

•

Now, THE PAST TWO evenings, she'd lit the candles after supper while she sat writing last-minute Christmas cards.

She had not written to many of her friends since Phillip's death almost a year and a half before. She told them she'd decided to stay on in Haïti, and that she continued to manage the embassy's commissary. The new political officer was a young man, she told them, very nice, but Ambassador Merriman had told her, several times, how he often wished for someone with Phillip's experience and tact.

She paused from time to time to look at the cathedral and admire it. It was hard to believe it was the work of such a young boy. He might have been ten or eleven, or he might have been older. Haïtian children, often undernourished, could be small for their age.

The cathedral made her think of what Christmas had been

for *her* when she was a child. They'd always had a huge blue spruce at home, and the house had smelled of bayberry candles, pine boughs and her mother's braided Christmas bread. Every Christmas she and her sister, Eloise, received new slippers. They'd leave the slippers on the hearth so they'd be warm when she and Eloise came in from playing in the snow.

But it made her uncomfortable to think about her childhood. She was fifty-one, a widow, and it seemed important she remember that—as though the fact demanded concentration. She preferred to examine such things from a distance, preferred the simplicity of the past, but she felt besieged now by the present, felt wary of her ordinary days. She watched time pass as if, by watching, she could prevent that one moment when the accumulated loss of years spilled over, changing everything. That's what you're left with by a sudden death, she thought.

When she looked at herself in the mirror, saw the gray streaks in her short, brown hair, the creases forming around the corners of her grayish-blue eyes, the way her mouth had become a thin line in her plumpening oval face, she was both startled and comforted: startled that she had expected to see something else, comforted that she hadn't. She was fifty-one, a widow. She held that definition in her mind, afraid, perhaps, that in forgetting it she might cease to be anyone at all.

Eloise had called from Evanston the night before. She and Carl and their two girls would leave for England, Christmas Day.

"Are you sure you'll be all right, Marcy? I hate to think you'll be alone on Christmas."

"I won't be alone. I'm having dinner with the Tomlinsons. I told you. Their son and daughter-in-law will be here from New Jersey."

"I wish you would come with us."

"I'll be fine. Wish everyone a merry Christmas for me."

She had then hung up the phone and gone into the kitchen. She'd poured a glass of water from the bottle in the refrigerator, not quite getting the door shut so that it swung open again as she stood over the sink to drink. Above the sink a small lizard clung to the outside of the window screen, its green underside luminous in the refrigerator's light.

This would be the second Christmas she had spent in Haïti. Christmas before last she and Phillip had gone to see his mother, and the year before that she'd been with Eloise's family. She could have gone to England with them this year, but it would have been expensive. She thought staying in Haïti for Christmas was another sign that she had made a life for herself here, although no one seemed to doubt that except her.

Remaining in Haïti was practical. She liked her house and was sure she could stay on at the commissary as long as she wanted to continue working.

"What would I do in the States?" she'd told Eloise. "I couldn't get a job, and I don't have friends there. I can live much more comfortably here for much less money."

"Besides," she'd added, "I've been living in tropical climates for eighteen years. I could never again get used to those Chicago winters."

It was true she could live cheaply here. She was used to having servants, too. Cleo did the laundry and housecleaning and most of the cooking. She had Phillip's insurance, his Foreign Service pension and the money he'd invested, and she had her share of the money from her parents' house. It was enough.

Her lease would be up in six months, and she would have to decide if she should renew it or if she should make an offer to buy this house. She'd always thought she and Phillip would decide where they would stay after he retired. Now she had to make the decision for herself.

They'd lived in eight foreign countries in twenty-six years. They couldn't decide where to buy a house in the States. Washington, where Phillip might, eventually, be posted? Near his mother in New Haven? Or her family in Evanston?

Phillip had grown up in a small town in Connecticut. It was the best kind of place to grow up, he'd often said. That was the kind of place he'd like to live when he retired. Theirs was not the kind of life for children, he used to say, and she agreed. He was always so sure of things, so definite. She thought that she was weak because she wasn't like that. He hadn't cheated her of anything. Why, then, did she feel she had lost something enormous? She envied Eloise. Is that what she had wanted for herself? Maybe now she did. And thirty years ago? She didn't know.

The Tomlinsons would be leaving in another year. She had other friends, would make other friends, but still she was afraid of being left behind. Her fear had the strange effect of making her calm. Everyone else interpreted this as courage.

•

WEDNESDAY WAS MARCELLA'S DAY off and she was having Sonia Tomlinson to lunch. Sonia was her best friend, the wife of the Economic Attaché. She was ten years older than Marcella, a Brit who had met her American husband during World War II, when she was a nurse and he a pilot.

"No, I didn't nurse him back from war wounds," she'd cheerfully explain to anyone who hadn't heard the story.

"Word went round they'd brought in a Yank who'd fallen out a top window of a double-decker bus. I had to go see him myself to find out how he ever managed it."

Jack Tomlinson would scowl and disapprovingly rattle the ice cubes in his tumbler of gin when she told this story, an act that always made Marcella laugh, no matter how many times she'd seen it.

Marcella had hoped to have lunch on the balcony, but it had rained that morning and the chairs and table were still wet. She told Cleo they would eat in the dining room instead.

Cleo had moved the cathedral to the low boy when she'd set the table, and Sonia walked right over to it.

"What a beautiful *fanal!*" she said, bending down to look at the rose window.

Marcella smiled, but said nothing. Usually she was eager to show off any purchase to Sonia, but now she wished Sonia would not examine the thing too closely.

"Oh, it really is *perfect*," Sonia went on. "I don't think I've ever seen one quite so nice." She gave Marcella an accusatory smile. Or so it seemed to Marcella.

"I bought it from a boy on Lalue the other night. There were a bunch of children selling them and I thought I ought to have one for the holidays."

"Well, as usual you chose the best. I have one that's a gingerbread house, but it's not nearly so nice. It must be lovely at night, with the candles lit."

"Yes," Marcella said, pulling her chair out from the table. "You must be eager to see Tom and Valerie. How long will they stay?"

·

LATER THAT AFTERNOON MARCELLA sat on her balcony and tried to read. She kept looking up from her book. The sky was full of silvery blue clouds. The ocean was gray beneath their shadows: flat, and finely etched with lines. Through the palms and mahogany trees she could just see part of the cathedral downtown, the white-washed stucco catching sun between the clouds. Its two bell towers were capped with pink cupolas, a delicate color, like anemones or the insides of seashells.

She thought again how pleasant it was to be in the hills, where there was always a breeze and the nights were cool enough to keep away mosquitoes. Her cobblestone street ended at the top of the hill, where the President had his villa. Sharing a street with the President meant that the electricity was rarely out for more than a short time and the phone was more reliable than at many of her friends' houses. But it could be an annoyance. Truckloads of soldiers went up and down the hill at all hours of the day and night. When it rained, the trucks' tires would slide and screech against the wet cobblestones, the gears would grind, and the engines would strain frantically for traction. On those rainy nights she'd often wake up to that noise and to the smell of burning diesel.

Across the street, a long, low wall was covered now with red poinsettias, the only natural clue in that tropical climate that it was nearing Christmas. She remembered the potted poinsettias her mother set around the house in Evanston every Christmas.

She heard children, then, coming up the hill. They were from the Catholic school, the girls in blue and gray plaid skirts and neat white blouses, the boys with shirttails hanging out from their navy pants. They joked and chased each other. Some carried metal lunch boxes decorated with American cartoon and movie characters: Snoopy, Darth Vader, Mickey Mouse. The parents must have bought the boxes in Miami. Marcella went into the house to find a cigarette.

A short time after Phillip died she'd started smoking. Because she didn't want anyone to know she smoked, she didn't buy her cigarettes at the commissary. In the evenings, about once a week, after Cleo had finished the supper dishes and gone home, she'd go downstairs to the gate. There was a boy who stayed around there, usually sitting against the poinsettia wall. His name was Max and he was maybe eight or nine years old. Marcella didn't know, but she presumed he lived in the ravine, where there was a community of tin and cardboard houses and where she could see cooking fires at night and smell burning charcoal and hear men and women laughing.

She would give Max a *gourde* to get her cigarettes. A *gourde* was twenty cents, enough to buy five cigarettes.

She'd tell him to buy three, or sometimes four, and he'd walk to the corner where a girl sold Chiclets, hard candy and cigarettes out of a shallow basket. Marcella would let the boy keep what change was left, the nickel and pennies or the extra cigarettes if that's what he wanted. It was silly, she knew, to buy a few at a time like this. At first she was afraid to have full packs around the house, but these were the local brand, *Comme Il Faut,* and they were strong and bitter. She didn't much like the taste and told herself that alone would ensure she didn't smoke more than a few. But she liked the routine, enjoyed the small intrigue of sending the boy to do an errand for her.

Coming back to the balcony to smoke, she began to think of the boy who made the cathedral. She wished she'd had a better look at him, his clothes. Then she could have judged his poverty. She wondered how long it had taken him to cut and trim, paste and smooth. She wondered where he got the tissue paper and the scissors. He hadn't spoken French, so she didn't know if he was schooled. But where else, but a school, could he have found supplies to make it?

It was a shame, she thought, that she had only given him a

dollar. Perhaps he'd made others and was able to sell them for more. Surely if he took them around to the hotels the tourists would buy them.

·

THAT NIGHT SHE DROVE down Lalue and through the surrounding streets. She drove through wealthy, hillside neighborhoods and downtown, where people were asleep on the steps of the Cathedral, and in the empty stalls of the Iron Market. The windows of the stores along Lalue were dark, but fluorescent light spilled out the open doors of the Green Cross pharmacy, and in street-front *borlettes* people stood beneath bare light bulbs and checked their tickets against the winning numbers scrawled on chalkboards. Near the waterfront she turned onto the road to Carrefour, the enormous slum, and smelled the gritty charcoal in the air and the stench left after rain turned roads into a thick, black mixture of mud and sewage. Eventually, she turned around and drove back up Lalue again toward Pétion-Ville. Twice she saw a small boy carrying a *fanal*, but when she slowed she saw that it was not the same boy.

She had not expected to find him but she had done what she could. Would she even have known him if she'd seen him?

After she showered and put on water for tea, she went into the dining room and saw the cathedral. She sat down at the table and inspected it. Two windows on one side were not exactly parallel, and on the other side one window was slightly taller than the other and not perfectly symmetrical. Of course he'd only made the one *fanal*. Its imperfections seemed, to her, a proof of this.

She imagined him as he was making it, the cardboard and paper spread out across a table, his face brought close to his hands as he worked, each detail a complete creation, wholly absorbing, as though the cathedral itself was too big a thing to take in all at once. She could see the scraps of colored paper reflected, like a kaleidoscope, in his dark eyes. That night, for the first time since she'd purchased the *fanal*, she didn't light the candles but instead took her book and a cup of tea to bed with her.

·

FRIDAY NIGHT WAS CHRISTMAS Eve. The Tomlinsons invited her for eggnog and rum punch and Marcella met Valerie and Tom. Both looked tired from their long day of traveling. Marcella left around nine-thirty and Sonia told her they'd eat dinner at two o'clock the next day. But she said Marcella should come over whenever she was up and felt like getting out.

"We'll be up early, I think. At our age it's hard to change habits, even for Christmas," she said.

When Marcella got home, she noticed Max standing by the poinsettia wall. Had he been waiting for her? She rolled down her window and asked him to open her gate.

He ran across the road, swung the wrought-iron gate out into the street and waited while Marcella pulled into the driveway.

"*Merci*, Max," she said as she got out of the car. He stood outside the gate, saying nothing. "*Attends*," she told him. *Wait*. She went to her door and stood under the porch light to see into her purse. From her wallet she pulled out five orange bills, five-*gourde* notes, a dollar each, then walked back to where the boy stood waiting. She rolled the bills into a cylinder and handed it to him.

"*Pour toi*," she said. "*Joyeux Noël*."

He didn't look at her or at the bills, but held them in the closed hand by his side. "*Merci*," he said. "*Bon Noël*."

Why was he out here alone, she wondered. Did he *have* a family?

She almost asked, then thought she'd better not. "*Attends ici*," she said, "OK?"

She was halfway down the stairs when she remembered she'd forgotten something, and set the cathedral on the steps. She turned back, thinking of the book of matches on the counter. He would need those, too.

Gene Pool

THE WOMAN AHEAD OF me in line likes my glasses.

"*So* cool," she says.

I return her smile and nod, acknowledging the compliment.

"I've never needed glasses," she says. "Twenty-twenty vision. Both my sons? Same thing."

"Wonderful," I say.

There's one barista and a woman at the register, seven customers ahead of me, and four more waiting for their orders to be filled. I haven't been inside a Starbucks in at least five years, but I can see that nothing's changed.

"A few years back?" the woman says, "I had my DNA done."

"Oh?"

"Turns out I'm carrying the female warrior Neanderthal gene!"

Roll with it, I tell myself. You're in L.A.

"I've always known," she says, "on some subconscious level. DNA analysis was just the cherry on the cake."

She means the *icing*, but I don't correct her.

"Anyway," she says, "the perfect vision thing? I'm sure you know Neanderthals were *hunters*."

She's my age—early fifties, possibly a few years younger—dressed for golf or tennis, and at least 6'4". It occurs to me she might be trans.

"I did *not* know that," I say. "Warriors and hunters, too? That doesn't leave a lot of market share for non-Neanderthals."

She laughs. "I never thought of *that*." She's giving me a closer look now, re-assessing. I can tell she likes me. I'm trying to remember if Neanderthals were tall.

"They stalked their prey at night! Your eyes had better be exceptionally good. Else you won't be bringing home much bacon."

"Eat the bacon," I say, "or the bacon will eat you."

"Here's the give-away," she says, and taps her forehead.

Her meaning isn't clear to me. I wait.

"*Un-us-u-ally* prominent. The *brow*. Both my sons? Same thing."

Her brow looks anything but prominent to me, but who am I to say? The physiognomy of warrior Neanderthals is well outside my area of expertise.

The line is moving, but I'm still four customers away from ordering my latté.

Maybe I should skip it. My father's at his bank across the parking lot, and soon I'll need to rescue the young Korean woman helping him. She's patient, but my father—a civil engineer—will take advantage of a captive listener, especially a pretty one. If I leave him long enough he will, inevitably, begin to talk to her about the properties of fly ash—a subject deeply interesting to him, but one unlikely to excite his listener.

"Boy, this line is slow!" the woman with the brow says. She smiles as if she's just said something clever, but the balding man in front of her is not amused.

"It's always slow," he says. "Get used to it."

"Okay," she says. "I beg to differ."

I wonder if the counter help is being slow on purpose. A second barista has arrived and is observing what the first is doing, while not doing anything himself. The woman at the register stops taking orders long enough to speak to him.

"I have people waiting for their drinks," she says. "Is something wrong?"

"Whatever happened to civility?" the woman with the brow says to the man in front of her. "I'm sorry if my small talk is annoying you. But that is *no* excuse for rudeness."

"I'm not on the clock," the dud barista tells the woman at the register.

"Oh," the woman with the brow says. "That's not good."

"You're more than right," the man in line says. "I was rude. I'm sorry. Order anything you like. I'll pay."

The woman at the register says—patiently, imploringly—to Dud Barista, "Please clock in. We need you." She must be all of twenty-two and handling the situation like a pro. Grace under pressure. Hemingway would be impressed.

"Sure thing," says Dud, and pushes through the swinging doors into the kitchen.

Now I'm thinking of the poor Korean woman at the bank. I ought to take her something—not coffee, but a muffin or a cup of orange juice—to thank her for her patience with my father.

Or I could just walk across the parking lot and take him off her hands.

"Apology accepted," the woman with the brow says to the man ahead of her, "and thank you for the offer, but I'll buy my own."

She turns to me and rolls her eyes. Her brow is, in fact, unusually prominent.

Through the plate glass window I can see a young man at the corner of El Toro and Paseo de Valencia; he's waiting for the light to change.

"Hey," I say. "Isn't that the guy who was going to clock in?"

Everyone in line agrees: that *is* the guy. Dud Barista. M.I.A.

"There's his apron," says the man who's sorry he was rude.

It is. It must be. Who else would leave a Starbucks apron draped across the wheelchair parked invitingly outside Adapt 2 It!—The One-Stop Shop for Those with Limited Mobility?

I excuse myself and go to fetch the apron. The waste of it, the carelessness, offends me, but I'm angered by the disrespect. I'm thinking of my father, who would never dream of throwing something out that someone else could use, who worked the crappiest of jobs to get through college because he had no one else to help him. Who, just this morning, told me he's a *lucky* man because he can afford the wheelchair he now relies on—the one we bought for him, on my last visit, at Adapt 2 It!

My father is a better, wiser man than I—for many reasons—and wouldn't be upset, as I am now. The young, he'd say, cannot imagine being old or limited in any way.

I bring the apron in and leave it on a stool behind the counter. The woman at the register says "Thank you," and I say, "I'd stay and help, but my father's waiting for me at his bank." I point to indicate the Union Bank across the parking lot.

The lone barista—younger than the one who's M.I.A.—is working both machines. He's got a rhythm going now: his timing crisp, his every move precise and purposeful. He's absorbed in what he's doing, executing at the highest level of proficiency. I know that feeling, being in a flow. There's nothing better. I could watch this young man do his job all day.

The woman with the brow says, "Bring your father here. I'll hold your place in line."

I say "thanks" and ask the woman at the register if I can help myself to a banana muffin and an orange juice "for the lady at the bank." I hold out a ten, but she shakes her head and indicates I'm welcome to the goods. I leave the money on the apron. "For the tip jar, then."

I take a muffin from the case; the woman with the brow steps out of line to get an orange juice and hands it to me when I come around the counter.

The man who's sorry he was rude says, "Tell me what you'd like. I'm buying. What about your dad?"

"You're very kind," I say, "but we might be a while. You needn't wait."

"I'm in no hurry," he says. "I'm not going anywhere."

The woman with the brow says, "I'm retired. And both my sons are in Afghanistan. I have all day."

I request a grande latté for myself, and a medium chai latté for Dad.

Before I leave, I thank them both again and ask if they might do me one more favor.

"Depends," the man says, furrowing his brow; there might be just the slightest trace of warrior Neanderthal in there.

"My father loves to meet new people. He won't talk about himself unless you ask, but he's a civil engineer. He's proud of things he's built in his career, and it would please him if you ask about them."

"*I'm* an engineer," the man says, "Or was. Retired. I bet we have a lot in common."

"Hurry," says the woman, "or your lattés will be cold when you get back."

"One more thing," I say. "It may sound odd."

One of the espresso makers hisses and emits a cloud of steam—the lone barista doesn't miss a beat.

"Go on," the woman says. "One more thing?"

"Ask my dad about the properties of fly ash."

My Fame

AT FIRST MY FRIENDS were pleased for me. They said things like, "It's about time!" and "Couldn't happen to a nicer guy." Then they stopped calling.

I had new friends, of course. Some stayed in touch a week or more, then disappeared. Others came and went the same day. *GQ* sent Gore Vidal to find out what makes me tick; I was asked to take a speaking part in Quentin Tarantino's new romantic comedy; a major television network wanted me to host the Emmies, but I had to turn them down because the Pope was giving me a medal that same week.

Sports Illustrated offered to pay handsomely for my commentary on the making of that year's swimsuit edition. Camille Paglia let it be known that she wanted me.

I was the topic of the week on *Crossfire*.

Journalists pretended to admire my work, then described me as a hack in print. Just before we went on air Katie Couric offered me another cruller. Then her eyes grew hard and cold. "Do you feel at all responsible," she said, the camera rolling, "for the crack-addicted children out there whose torture of small animals started only after your book hit best-sellerdom?"

I turned down offers to appear on other shows. I declined comment, spurned interviews. This didn't stop the stories. My former mailman told *Inside Edition* that I had for years played chess-by-mail with Dr. Jack Kevorkian. The car wash attendant said I only tipped a dollar though I must have been aware that it would take much more than that to pay for her son's liver transplant. Someone I had never heard of professed to have spent time with me assembling pipe bombs in the back booth of a Charlestown, Massachusetts bar.

Gore Vidal's article said I had been spotted on a yacht in the Greek Islands nude sunbathing with Iraqi President Saddam Hussein.

One day the phone rang and a man said, "I am the attorney representing your ex-wife."

"But I never married," I said, "I don't have an ex-wife."

"Doesn't matter," he said, "This is going to cost you plenty."

The car wash attendant sued. She claimed sophisticated DNA analysis showed I was the father of her ailing child. She wept on *60 Minutes*. She looked directly at the camera and said, "Come home. Your baby and I need you."

The SEC sent letters saying that a former business partner had provided documented evidence of my involvement in insider trading. A new book about Nixon quoted him as saying I kicked Pat when she was down. J.D. Salinger denounced me as a plagiarist. I began to get cold calls from Betty Ford.

Alan Dershowitz's secretary said she'd been instructed not to put my calls through under any circumstance.

Liz confessed it was my fling with Larry that broke up their marriage. Paula Jones said I had approached her in a hotel lobby and requested that she autograph a private part of my anatomy that she could identify by a "distinguishing characteristic." A pit boss at the Hard Rock Cafe and Casino, in Las Vegas, reported that I had dropped tens of thousands at the baccarat table, then thrown my Stoli in the dealer's face. Rush Limbaugh said I was the one who'd hooked him on cigars.

The National Enquirer ran a photo which it claimed showed me emerging from Lyle Lovett's hotel room at sunrise.

The presidential candidates competed to denounce me.

One suggested I was Willie Horton's long lost twin. I made the cover of *Time* magazine, my image morphing into that of former L.A. police detective, Mark Fuhrman.

Then, one day, it stopped. Someone had made off with two truckloads of weapons-grade plutonium from a secret military outpost in Sun Valley, Idaho. Rumor had it that the stuff was on its way to Teheran. That same day the cast of *Friends* was lost in a freak accident while filming a commercial for America Online.

The phone stayed quiet eight days. Then it rang. "Hold for Mr. Stone," the operator said.

"Call me Ollie," Mr. Stone said. "How about I make the movie of your life?"

Le Bon Chapeau

THE *CAMION* WAS FILLING up with passengers, and Alix was glad he'd arrived early enough to take a seat by a window. The window's inner panel was pulled down, leaving the window open at the top. A bee was trapped in the bottom, between the two panes of glass. Alix looked at the brownish yellow fur of its underside and put his finger on the window at the spot. The glass was warmer than he'd expected; that, and the way its hard smoothness contradicted the velvet bee, made him pull his hand away. The bee bobbed unsteadily in the narrow space, beating a faint, violent racket against the glass.

Alix had traveled to Cap-Haïtien the day before, and had stayed overnight. Now he felt relieved and happy to be returning home. The *camion* would take him from Le Cap to Ouanaminthe; from Ouanaminthe he would go on foot and horseback to his village.

He counted eleven other *camions* parked haphazardly around the open dirt lot that served as a depot. The *camions* were painted red, green, yellow and blue. Some were covered with careful geometric designs, others with irregular, ill-matched areas that overlapped so that it was impossible to tell which had been the original color.

The name of a city or town was painted on the cab of each truck, above the windshield: Gonaïves, Port-au-Prince, Ft. Liberté. Everything looked brilliant in the late morning sun: the blue-gray sea, the other *camions*, even the people. A breeze came through the open window. Alix smelled the dark, fermented ocean; diesel fumes; *griots* fat dripping onto hot coals. A woman walked beneath his window carrying a basket full of small paper bags soaked through in spots with oil. He smelled sweet, fried *bananes figue*, and wished he had money to buy some. But he'd spent his money on a hat.

He took the hat off and held it in his lap. It was made of yellow straw and had a high crown with a crease down the center and a brim that curled up along the sides but lay flat in front to keep the sun from his eyes. The straw had a clean, dry smell. The strands were woven tightly, intersecting in tiny ridges that made his fingers tingle when he ran them across the surface. It was a fine hat, a man's hat. *Bananes figue* is nothing special, he thought, but a hat like this is worth having.

Father Jerome had given him enough money, when he left the village, to buy his ticket and some food. But this morning he'd eaten rice, bread and papaya at the Oblate Mission. That would last until he got home. He was anxious to start. By the time he got to the base of the mountain, where Sinon would meet him with the horse, it would be dark.

A man outside tossed cardboard suitcases and straw baskets to a man on the roof of the *camion*. A brown and white goat, its legs bound, lay quietly on the ground. As soon as the goat was tied down on top of all the other baggage the *camion* could leave.

Alix's satchel sat on the floor next to his feet. Inside the satchel were the few small items the Mission priest was sending back to Father Jerome: two letters, batteries for the radio, and a gift-wrapped pouch that the Mission priest had told him contained pipe tobacco. One letter was from Canada where Father Jerome's family lived. The other was from the Mission priest. Alix knew that Father Jerome would be pleased to receive these things, and he again felt happy he'd been chosen to make the trip. The papers he'd brought with him were requests for supplies for the parish and the school, Father Jerome had told him. Brother Manzio would have brought the papers, but he had the stomach flu. Father Jerome couldn't come himself because it was Holy Week. An older student who had made the trip once before had gone across the border this year to cut cane with the men.

"I could wait until Brother Manzio is well enough to travel," Father Jerome had told Alix, "but there's no reason to put it off. Besides, this is a chance for you to see the Mission school."

Alix thought he would like to live in Le Cap, where he could swim in the ocean and wear a uniform to school. He was already in the last stage in the parish school, though he would not be thirteen until July. The other three students at his level were already fifteen. Brother Manzio said he was a good student, and he knew he could read French better than the others. Father Jerome told him if he wanted to go to the Mission school it might be possible to arrange a scholarship and to find a place for him to live with a family where he could work in exchange for his room and meals.

Maybe the letter in his satchel said whether he would be allowed to come to the school. He wasn't sure that was what he wanted. If he went to the school, his mother would be left alone in the village. Because he was his mother's only son, he wanted to take care of her. He thought of reaching into the bag and opening the letter, but instead reached for the hat and put it on his head, careful not to push it out of shape.

When he turned away from the window, Alix saw a woman sitting on the bench beside him. The bench was long enough for three people, but this woman was large. There was no room left for another person to sit down. She put her straw market bag on the bench between them and set about rearranging its contents, moving her hands around inside and making it bulge and twist as though it contained something alive. She wore a long skirt that had green and black swirls on it, and a man's green shirt. The scarf around her hair was made from the same material as the skirt; her earrings looked like pieces of copper hammered flat. Her skin was dark and smooth as a seed.

When she finished with the bag she set it on the floor next to Alix's satchel, and rested her hands in her lap. Her fingers, Alix saw, were long and her nails, cut short, were like small, pink shells. On each finger she wore at least one ring: some were plain bands, others had designs etched into them. One ring was in the shape of a serpent biting its own tail. The woman crossed her right hand over her left and rubbed the middle and index fingers against each other, clicking their rings together in a quick, impatient rhythm.

The driver started the engine of the *camion* and closed the door. In another minute they were moving slowly across the dirt lot, raising dust that floated through the open window. Alix felt a tap on his shoulder. He turned around.

"Close the window until we reach the paved road," the woman said.

Alix pushed up on the lower half of the window with one hand, but it wouldn't move. He tried pushing with both hands. When the window still wouldn't move, the woman leaned over and took hold of the frame. She pulled it towards her and lifted. The window then closed easily. Alix gave her an embarrassed smile; then he remembered the bee. When he turned, he saw the bee launch itself from the edge of the window frame and for a moment hang in the air a few inches from his face. He slapped at it, but missed. The bee flew to the window and lit on the glass. Before Alix could think of how to kill it, the woman leaned across, pinched the bee between her thumb and forefinger and let it fall to the floor. A yellow smudge remained on the glass. The woman cleaned her fingers with a tissue, carefully and slowly, as she might have done while polishing her rings.

"Do not like bees," she said. "Don't like no thing that wants to bite me. Let him try, he'll see what he gets."

Alix moved as if to make himself more comfortable on the bench, and crushed the bee with his sandal, to be sure it was dead. He turned back to the window. He wanted to wipe the glass clean, but thought the woman might be watching; so he left his hands in his lap and let the edge of the road outside run past his eyes like water in the river.

·

THE LAND ALONG THE coast was flat; fields of dry, yellow sisal stretched across it like a dog's coarse coat. Alix saw mango trees in the distance, heavy-limbed and lit with flashes of green and orange fruit among their dark, wind-turned leaves. It was the season. He thought about the small, sweet mangoes his uncle had brought once from Jean-Rabel. Nowhere had Alix ever tasted mangoes so sweet as those, and his stomach tightened at the memory.

"We are on the paved road now," the woman said.

This time the window did not resist. The air came through in a gust. Alix took the hat off and held it in his lap. He ran the back of his hand across his forehead, which was slick with sweat. His scalp tingled with perspiration.

He had bought the hat from a man on the wooden foot bridge that led across a small inlet to the *camion* depot. Hats had been stacked one on top of another, and piled up against the side of the bridge, glowing like ripe fruit in the sun. Alix wondered how long it took to make so many hats. A few were dyed brown, or had bands of pink or green woven through them, but most were plain yellow straw. Some, the kind the merchant women wore, had fringes of uncut straw around their wide brims. But in an instant Alix saw the hat he wanted. When he tried it on, he was not surprised it fit. The man who made the hats looked up from the stool where he sat working.

"That is just the hat for you, *mon cher*. It will keep the sun and rain away, but bring the girls close." He'd laughed and called out to another man, across from them, to look.

Alix wasn't sure if they were making fun of him. He took the hat off and turned it over in his hands, then put it on again and walked over to the man on the stool.

"How much?" he asked.

"One *gourde* only, *mon cher*."

Alix had only two *goudin*, half a *gourde*. "I don't have that much," he said. He reached into his shorts, to the secret pocket his mother had sewn along the inside band, and pulled out the two coins. They were black and worn thin at the edge, their denomination clear only by their size. Holding them in his palm, Alix suddenly felt foolish. He was about to put the coins back in his pocket and return the hat when the man took them out of his hand. The man examined the coins, as if they might be worthless, then folded his hand around them and shook them like dice. He looked at Alix, studying Alix's face as he had the coins. His eyes were dark in the shade of his own hat's brim. Alix thought he might throw the two coins back at him, or over the bridge into the water. Instead, he stood and put them in his pocket.

"This hat is made well for you," he said. "A hat should give a man authority."

He straightened the hat on Alix's head, and bent the brim

down a little in front until he seemed satisfied with the way it looked.

"Good day, *mon cher*," he said, and sat back on his stool.

•

"YOU HAVE VISITED YOUR family in Le Cap?"The woman was speaking to him. Alix, still thinking of the man on the bridge, looked at her. She had a pleasant face.

"My family is in Trinité," he said.

"That place I don't know. You go to Ouanaminthe?"

"Ouanaminthe and then some more."

"A long trip, that is. You will stop someplace tonight, I hope."

"No. I'll be home tonight."

The woman looked at him. It was a kind of appraisal, Alix thought, as though she were deciding whether or not to purchase goods. He looked at her hands, her many rings.

"I would worry to send a boy on such a long trip by himself," she said. "Your family must be happy to have a boy to take care of their affairs in the city."

Alix did not like to be called a boy, but he was glad this woman saw that he was someone who could be trusted with important business.

"The priest sent me, to take some documents," he said, certain this would impress her.

"To send a boy for that!" she said, and brought her hands together. "Let this priest go himself, if he has business with documents."

Alix wondered how she could think a priest would have time during Holy Week for such a trip.

"I *wanted* to come," he said. "To see the Mission school. I might be sent there to study."

"Yes they want to send you to this school, to make another

priest. There are not enough of them, just yet, to give every-body in the country trouble."

Alix had never heard anyone speak that way about a priest—not even Sinon, who made jokes about everyone, and called Brother Manzio a bald nun. Sinon, he thought, was just ignorant, but an adult should know to be more respectful.

"If you put on a priest's white robes," the woman said, leaning forward and touching his arm, "don't forget the skin they cover is black."

She sat back and closed her eyes. Alix thought she intended to sleep. Then he heard the rings make a metallic clacking sound as she rubbed them, one against the other. The woman opened her eyes and said, as if addressing someone else, "I do not travel at night. During the day, if you see a dog, you know it is a dog, and an owl asleep in a tree is only that. At night, the dog or the owl could be the disguise of a *bokor* who has been paid by your enemies to harm you." She smoothed her skirt with her hands, catching one ring on a loose thread. She leaned over, squinting at the spot until she worked the ring free. Then she settled back and closed her eyes again.

Most of what Alix knew of *voodoo* he had learned from Sinon. Sinon was sixteen and had come to the parish house two years before, hungry and claiming he had no family. Father Jerome had given him a room to live in and, in exchange, Sinon took care of the parish garden and the ani-mals. Sometimes Alix listened to Sinon's stories of *houngans* and zombies and the way the *loa* came down to the rhythm of the drums. Sinon said one time he had watched a man possessed by Damballah, the serpent, wrap himself around the trunk of a tall palm and slither to the top without using his hands or feet.

•

THE ROAD SEEMED LONGER going home. After several hours there was nothing new to see. The woman was asleep and the drone of the truck's engine made Alix drowsy. Every now and then they stopped, and passengers got off and claimed their things. But the stops were brief. The *camion* pulled off the highway for one stop, jolting hard against the pavement's edge. Alix sat up, startled for a moment by his surroundings. He had been asleep. The *camion* was half empty; the woman was gone. He stretched his legs out on the bench and slept.

When he woke they were in Ouanaminthe. The sun was still above the mountain. Glad for the chance to walk, Alix picked up the satchel, checked to make sure the hat was still on his head, and hurried up the road. A few hundred feet from where the *camion* stopped, the pavement ended. It was harder to walk on the soft dirt. Sinon was probably already waiting. He would have tethered the horse to the mimosa tree and would be sitting against a rock, flipping pebbles at the animal's haunches to make it flinch.

It took an hour for Alix to reach the spot where he would meet Sinon. By then the sun had gone behind the mountain. The moon, almost full, was rising, and the mountains were like jagged pieces fallen from the sky. Alix knew this road well, but several times he came around a curve expecting to be at his destination only to find that he had misjudged. He did not like walking by himself at night, but soon enough he would be in Sinon's company. He walked faster.

Comforted by the sound his sandals made slapping against his heels, he made them slap more loudly.

Finally, when he saw the black shape of the mimosa tree ahead, his pulse quickened with relief. He slowed his pace, not wishing to appear too hurried. As he came closer, he did not see the horse, or Sinon. He felt a pang. What if Sinon hadn't come? Then he would have to walk up the mountain by himself. He came closer to the tree and said, weakly at first, "*Allo*?" and then, feeling foolish, he said it again, louder.

"*Allo*, Alix," came the reply from behind him.

Sinon had meant to startle him, but Alix was glad to hear Sinon's voice, and the familiar sound of his uneven gait as he approached. Sinon's left leg was atrophied. When he came closer, Alix could see his face. Sinon wore, always, the same expression of indifference, thinking it made him look intelligent. This, even though he could not read or speak French, and had never been to Le Cap.

Sinon untied the horse and led it over to the rock where he'd been sitting. He climbed from the rock onto the horse, and then Alix climbed on behind. Before they started, Alix pushed the hat down on his head, and made sure to get a good grip on the satchel.

Sinon rode with his hands resting against the horse's neck, holding the reins loosely. Alix pressed his knees tightly against the horse's sides. When his leg touched one of the slick spots where the horse had rubbed the hair off, he moved it away.

The horse was old, and climbed slowly, rocking with each step. As the road became steeper, the horse's sides bellowed with the effort of its breathing. Its hooves cracked sharply against the small rocks in the road. On their left, the mountainside was hidden in the darkness, the shapes of bushes and boulders indistinct. To their right, Alix could sense the emptiness where the mountain fell away, and he could hear the soft, brushing sound of warm air turning round inside the valley like a dog settling to sleep.

"They say a *loup-garou* has been in the valley and killed a cow," Sinon said.

"They found the cow?" Alix wondered if there was such a

thing as a *loup-garou*. How could a man turn into a wolf? But he remembered what the woman said about *bokors* disguised as dogs or owls.

"Yes. Its throat was torn open."

He thought he heard a sound behind them, but he listened for a minute and decided it was only the sound of the horse breathing.

"Someone was probably seeking revenge on the owner, and killed it," he said.

"Maybe so."

As they rode, Alix was aware of all the sounds around him. He could hear Sinon's bad leg flop against the horse's side, and his breathing, and the horse's hooves against the road. But there was another sound. It might have been an echo. He listened carefully to see if it was only that, a familiar sound made strange by the echo following so closely. It was a rhythmic, clicking sound, like metal hitting metal. He thought about the woman's rings.

"Sinon," he said, "do you hear something behind us?"

"Do you think the *loup-garou* is waiting in the bushes to jump out at us?" Sinon spoke mockingly, but he pulled on the reins to stop the horse. They sat still, listening. The horse lowered its head, resting. Alix could hear nothing but the sound of his own breathing, and the horse's, and Sinon's. Then he heard a different sound that might have been an animal, emerging from the brush onto the road. He turned to look behind them. Something stirred in the brush beside them then, and they heard wood break.

Sinon leaned over the horse's neck and dug his heels into its sides. "*Allez!*" he urged. The horse, jolted unexpectedly from its torpor, kicked forward. Alix almost fell over backward. He grabbed hold of Sinon's shirt and pulled himself upright. Then he held tight, his arms around Sinon's waist. As it trotted, the horse seemed to be trying to shake off its load so that Alix was bouncing on the animal's back and being shifted from side to side.

In the moment after he'd recovered from his fear and surprise he felt the hat slip toward the back of his head. He let go of Sinon and reached for it. Just then he sensed the satchel slipping from his other hand. He grabbed onto the satchel with both hands, clutching it to his stomach as though he feared it might fight free of him.

Bent forward, with his head against Sinon's side, he could hear the rapid, metallic clicking of the rings where the reins attached to the bit, and saw, behind him, the straw hat tumbling across the road, and then, as if lifted by an unseen hand, fly toward the mountain's black edge.

His Red Heaven

IN HEAVEN, V.I. LENIN plays electric bass. The band is called Satori. They play R&B, light rock, a sentimental ballad here and there to mix it up. Every now and then they'll throw the audience off guard with a *cumbia*, a Scott Joplin rag, or classic Charlie Patton.

It's not the way you'd think it would be here: unlimited supplies of everything, no wear or grime. The mike stand's held together with electrician's tape; the P.A.'s an assemblage of frayed wires, bungee cords and mismatched scraps of plywood. Lenin himself makes do with strings that give off muddy, thudding tones. In places where the brass wire is separating from the nylon core, he's brushed on a coat of clear nail polish—a trick he learned from the band's singer, Sylvio.

Things get old and torn and broken, don't work properly, but nothing ever seems to reach the point of failure and so nothing ever gets replaced. Lenin sometimes wonders if the shortages and questionable quality of goods are God's idea of karma. Months go by in which there's not a decent jar of mustard, or a radish, or a lump of sugar to be had. It's not that life in heaven isn't good. It is. It's just not all it was cracked up to be.

Sylvio's the band's big draw. The crowds come for the privilege of watching him ignore them. Every number is a private exorcism; the appalling intimacy of his phrasing on "Surrender" leaves them quaking in their seats. Sylvio's been known to walk off stage, mid-set, at the sound of one hand clapping.

Off stage he's an ordinary guy, no different from the rest of them. On stage he's the Bad Boy of the Apocalypse.

Lenin has good days and bad. He tries to focus on the bigger picture, not let day-to-day concerns consume him. But he worries that he's lost the discipline and fervor of his youth, the sense of purpose that once drove him. He tells himself it doesn't matter; there is nothing to be done here. No exigencies. Systems might be put in place, performance optimized around the margins. But, but, but…why rock the boat? In the face of insufficient indignation, revolution is beside the point.

He had trouble, early on, adapting to his situation. This was not, to say the least, what he expected. But after he sought counseling, he came to understand that he was merely acting out an old and comforting scenario that didn't fit his present circumstance. Once he recognized that these old patterns of behavior *never* worked in *any* circumstance, he started to relax. Soon enough, he wanted to fit in. That's how he hooked up with Sylvio.

He loves what he does. He loves the crowded club space, the dim light. He even loves the laughable acoustics. An off night doesn't blunt his pleasure in performing. He finds, to his surprise, that he *likes* being in the shadows. For once, he's not the center of attention.

An eerie type of symbiosis sets in when a band has been around as long as this one has. He knows where Sylvio is going before Sylvio himself knows. Lenin gets there just ahead of him, lays down a note, a stone, where Sylvio can rest his weight. That's the very essence of his job. He's good at it.

Lately, there's been talk of touring. Putting down a few tracks in the studio to see where that might take the band. Lenin tells himself that it will never happen. No one wants to give up what they have now for some ill-defined chimera called success. He could drive things that way if he wanted, be the instigator and the impresario. But he knows those days are well behind him. He's content to leave them there.

Sylvio says he might, eventually, move on to other projects. He worries he'll go stale, or—worse—become a parody of himself without his knowing. He says the work of digging deeper, finding some authentic core of feeling—not a message, but a vibe—is hollowing him out.

Lenin listens. What else can he do? One day Sylvio will not show up. No warnings, no apologies. That's the day Satori will be finished. Done.

Lenin wonders what he'll do when that day comes, but quickly brings his thoughts back to the present. No point in trying to prepare for the unknowable. He's been down that road before, planning for a workers' paradise that never came. That kind of thinking never works. It never will.

He might be the first to tire. Would he keep going if the music wasn't giving him the satisfaction, or the sense of possibility, it does now? What would be the point? There might be other means of self-expression that he hasn't yet caught onto: levels of experience and knowing that are, for now, beyond his ken.

He can't concern himself with destinies—his own, or others', or the band's. Whatever comes, comes. His situation isn't of his making, and he must accept it. That's the best that he, or anyone, can do.

The Plagiarist

ONE MORNING, AFTER TWELVE years of writing fiction with small success, Townsend Beane produced a masterpiece.

The thing came out like one long exhalation: eight and one half pages, single-spaced; whole, complete, and unlike anything Beane had ever written.

He looked it over, once, then shut down his computer and went upstairs to make his lunch. This experience was unfamiliar, the results so unanticipated, that he didn't want to make too much of them too soon. First impressions rarely held against the more objective reading that came later.

Many times he'd thought what he was writing was the best thing he had ever written, that the breakthrough he had long desired and waited for had come, only to be disappointed when he gave the piece a second, presumably more objective, reading later.

As he went about his business for the day—his swing shift at the library, his counter job at the used bookstore downtown—he purposefully kept himself from thinking about the new pages he'd written. The next morning he read the piece again.

This time he recognized it as a work of genius. It was savage, succinct, and revelatory. It was old as fable, modern as the evening news. He went through it again, amazed. It wasn't perfect: he found two awkward phrases, a poorly chosen adjective, a paragraph that would be more effective coming closer to the end. Otherwise, he didn't see a single word that could be taken out. Every word was tied to every other: take one out and the story's edifice would fall in on itself.

Clearly the work had come from some deep part of himself

that he had hardly ever tapped. On a few, rare, occasions he'd produced work he felt was beyond what he was capable of doing, that the words weren't his, but had come from somewhere other than inside him, that he'd merely been the instrument the Muse had chosen for that day. But that had happened only with particular scenes, a stretch of dialogue or exposition that stood out in the context of a longer piece of work that, ultimately, didn't hold together.

Moments like these were what kept him going. If he was capable of producing those few brilliant paragraphs, the occasional, near-perfect scene, then perhaps he had it in him, after all, to write. He kept at it, in the process becoming ever more diligent, more disciplined, and wondering if he might arrive, eventually, at greatness, or at madness. Or both.

He spoke to no one about his writing. Editors at several literary magazines had seen his work and some wrote words of encouragement on letters of rejection. "Almost!" "Try us again!"

In twelve years he'd published seven stories: five in obscure quarterlies that had since gone out of business; two in reputable magazines that, while not glossies, were distributed nationally, and were well known among writers. One of those two stories had been cited as an "honorable mention" in an annual "Best Of."

That was the closest he had come to success.

This piece was something new and different and alarming. Reading it was like reading someone else's words. Where had this story been? Why had it come to him now? Who were these characters, unlike anyone he'd known in real life, and why was it that their voices came to him so clearly, so compellingly? What made these, of all the characters he'd ever written, seem so natural, so real?

Reading it again confirmed his earlier conclusion: the

piece was a masterwork of compression; emotion and social observation wedded in less than three thousand words; a commentary and a *cri de coeur*. It was old as Aesop, original as Borges, humane as Garcia-Marquez. It was a tiny story about seemingly inconsequential things, and it was as nearly perfect as anything he would ever write.

He doubted he would ever again write this well. Not in this life. How he'd stumbled on this hidden reservoir, he didn't know. He'd been given a gift from the gods. Unlikely they would visit him a second time.

And that would be all right. If this one short piece became what he was known for, his name, at least, would live on. This piece would speak to future generations as intelligibly as to his own. It was timeless, universal. It would appear in "Best Of" and be anthologized for years to come. College students and literary scholars would critique it. It would be a rarity— the one great piece by an otherwise obscure writer of the late twentieth century. That would be enough. Townsend would be satisfied with that.

·

As HE PUSHED HIS cart through the library stacks that afternoon, replacing books on shelves, he considered where he ought to send the piece. Who would pay the most? Where would it get the most exposure? Which, among the small universe of editors who had been kind to him, might he repay by sending them this gem?

He imagined seeing his name on the covers of the glossy magazines you buy at newsstands and at airport bookshops. How would it feel, to have so many people know his name, if only briefly? He would, after all, have his speck of fame, the sort of brief, illuminating flash emitted by a dying star, before he once again retreated into darkness and obscurity.

•

THE FOLLOWING DAY, READING through the piece again, he was more impressed with himself than ever. Not only was it unlike anything he'd ever written, it contained a level of insight he had chased for years, and hadn't found. It was devoid of cliché or sentimentality, of false feeling of any kind. It was a pure thing, as exact an expression of human longing and discouragement as language was capable of carrying.

But had he written it? Had he written this piece that was so beautiful, so moving? So unlike his style, his subject matter? So beyond his limitations?

What if he *hadn't* written it? Could it be some other writer's work, something that had stayed buried in his memory for years? What if some channel had opened between his subconscious and his memory and he had simply revived, in remarkable detail, the work of some earlier genius? Was it Babel? Poe? Turgenev? Porter? It couldn't have been Bierce, or Chekhov.

He set these thoughts aside and went off to work.

•

ALL THAT AFTERNOON HE couldn't shake this sense of queasiness and doubt. What if he had stolen it? What if the one great thing he'd ever write was copied from another writer? How humiliating it would be if he sent the piece out, only to have an editor send back a scathing response: "Dear Mr. Beane, Thank you so much for sharing Anton Makarenko's brilliant and well-known story with us...."

He was being paranoid. He'd look at it again, tomorrow, and see how he felt then.

•

THE NEXT DAY HE FELT more certain than he had the day before that this work could not have come from him. There was nothing of him in it. No remembered experience, no person he had ever known resembling the narrator, no detail of setting, no gesture, that he might actually have transcribed from life. It was so smooth, so polished, for a first draft. How could that have happened without so much as one false step, one misplaced word or unintended ambiguity?

Where could it have come from?

He got up from his desk and went upstairs. He examined volumes of short stories on his bookcase: Flannery O'Connor, Frank O'Connor, William Trevor, Alice Munro, Tobias Wolff, Barthelme, Borges, Garcia-Marquez, Joyce, Hemingway, Fitzgerald, Faulkner, Lawrence, Anderson, Welty, Cheever, Paley, Gass.

He emptied the shelf of his "Best Of" anthologies (a complete set, going back fifteen years) and looked through every table of contents for his title. If he had stolen the piece he likely would have stolen the title, too.

Nothing he found jogged his memory. He opened each book with dread, afraid his eye would spot the piece—his piece—only by a different author, written years before.

He returned to the basement and pulled out the cardboard boxes where he'd stored his college textbooks. He found anthologies from literature classes he had taken thirty years before. He skimmed their contents methodically, calmly. He took his time. He could not find what he was looking for.

But he was certain, now, more certain than he'd been before, that the piece he'd "written" was not his. He had remembered it. Inexplicable but true. He need only find the source, the writer's name, and then thank God he hadn't sent it out, which could have ruined him. Soon enough, he could go back to working on stories that were his alone, with their pathetic, inconsequential themes and stylistic quirks.

•

THAT AFTERNOON HE PARKED his cart among the shelves of short story anthologies on the library's second floor, and spent an hour browsing. Eventually the reference librarian came looking for him.

"Where have you been?" she asked. "There are five more carts that need to be shelved before closing."

That evening, at the bookstore, he left the counter unmanned while he looked through the floor-to-ceiling shelves of fiction, arranged alphabetically by author. He examined every single book, checking author and title against his memory, against his reading of his own short piece, to see if anything clicked, to confirm where he might have encountered the piece before. He made it through the "J"s by closing time and, after, locking the door and turning the sign to "Closed," stayed until the early hours of the morning, inspecting the remaining books.

•

THE FOLLOWING DAY HE showed up at the library four hours before his shift began. The reference librarian was surprised to see him. He told her he was doing research, then spent the extra time going through periodicals, scanning Tables of Contents, looking at back issues of seven or eight popular or literary magazines he regularly read, and several more he picked up only on occasion. He asked the periodicals assistant to retrieve back issues for him, going back two years.

When the time came to start his shift he'd come up empty.

•

FINALLY HE SENT THE piece out in a plain envelope with no return address and nothing on the manuscript that could identify its author. He sent it to the best-known, best-paying, most widely-read magazine in the country. And every week he checked the latest issue to see if his piece was there.

•

MONTHS PASSED AND HE forgot about it. He went back to writing his coming-of-age novel, a pathetic retread telling of a story that had been told a thousand times before, by a thousand writers, each better than he.

And then he died. The experience of having written something so magnificent, then doubting its origin, had so unhinged him that he'd started living in a distracted, foggy haze. One night the bookstore was held up by a young man with a goatee and wire-rimmed glasses—a young Chekhov, really. Beane was slow to open the register and the young man shot him in the face.

•

THE PIECE WAS PUBLISHED six weeks after Townsend Beane was cremated. The magazine's fiction editor explained to readers that the story had come to them through regular mail, in a plain manila envelope with nothing else included that would help them to identify its author. The envelope bore a Gary, Indiana postmark, but she had no way of knowing whether that was where the author lived, or if the writer— he, or she—resided elsewhere. The magazine's best research assistants tried for weeks to track down the story's author, using clues of style and subject matter the manuscript itself provided, with no plausible result.

A professor at Dartmouth had submitted the manuscript to linguistic forensic analysis, using sophisticated software she'd created that was widely used by major corporations and the FBI.

That program compared the manuscript, linguistically and stylistically, to the works of seven hundred well-known authors who were writing between the years 1895 and 2015. She had failed to find a likely author. There was no match.

"Somewhere out there in America," the editor's note concluded, "in Gary, Indiana, or in some other city, or some other town, an unknown master is at work, building narratives the way medieval craftsmen built cathedrals, producing, out of stone, effects as light as air. When those earlier masterpieces were completed, they, too, were left unsigned. Rare enough in the medieval world, much less in ours.

"We can only hope the writer of this piece might now be tempted to come forward and identify herself or himself, and receive the recognition he or she deserves. Barring that, we hope the writer is at work on some new manuscript, and that other manuscripts might someday come to light."

How I Met You

YOU WALK INTO A room. I am sitting at a table, reading *The Encyclopedia of Dogs*.

"The Komondor," you say, "was brought to Hungary a thousand years ago by nomadic Magyars."

I am looking at a picture of an Otterhound. Confused, I put my hand to my face. The book falls closed.

You come around the table. It's an ugly table, with steel legs and a green Formica top, like something from a laboratory. On one corner, near my right hand, someone has drawn a dragonfly in ink. It is exquisite, delicate, precise. The wings appear to hold light.

"Were you finished?" you ask.

You take off my glasses, fold them closed, and slip them in the pocket of your vest. Why would you have on a vest? A Tarot card peeks out from the other pocket: The Hanged Man.

"Yes," I say. "I think so."

"Good."

Is this going to get schmaltzy? Literary? Pornographic? I am suddenly afraid you will turn out to be a symbol. Nothing more.

I would do anything to keep you real. You have red hair. The eyebrow over your right eye turns up at one end, like a sickle, or a question mark lying on its back.

"What is a Magyar?"

You sit in the chair across from me. "Forget the Otterhound," you say. "It's not the dog for you."

You fold back the cuff of your blouse, showing me the

white skin of your wrist. A blue vein runs across the tendon there. The blouse: green silk with darker green leaves woven through the fabric. When you roll your sleeve up, though, the leaves remain, twined around your forearm.

I put my index finger to the blue vein in your wrist and trace the green vine running in among the leaves. I trace it up your arm, and down, and then I lay my hand in yours.

And when you turn your hand, I see the green vine snaking up my own arm, curving over bone and tendon, branching.

There, among the green leaves, is the dragonfly, the light.

Weather

RICH LAWSON DIDN'T OFTEN travel for his company, but when they asked if he would oversee an installation on the West Coast, he said yes, because he would have traveled anywhere to see his old friend, Martin. He flew to San Francisco on a Saturday, and that afternoon he drove a rental down to Monterey.

It was October. Already this year they'd had snow in Massachusetts; here, palm trees swept an empty sky. He leaned over the wheel, excited, giddy almost, with the idea of seeing Martin, seeing California, driving down an eight-lane highway full of clean and polished cars. Even the blue and yellow license plates looked waxed. Not a single fender eaten through by road salt.

This visit would be good for both of them. Rich needed time away from Carol; he realized, a little guiltily, how long he'd waited for an opportunity to get off by himself, and that was something he wanted to discuss with Martin. But he wasn't thinking only of himself; Martin needed him just then. The way Rich saw it Martin needed to be shaken up a bit, encouraged. He'd had a tough time recently but when you live in California there are reasons all around you to be happy. Rich meant to point them out. He could start with weather.

Martin had moved west two years before, around the time that Rich re-married, but things had not worked out the way he planned. The start-up software company he'd come to California to work for had gone under and he'd had to take a sales job at Computer Haus. Women were another story. Martin hadn't had a steady girlfriend since he moved to California.

The few times he had mentioned any one by name it was to say that he'd stopped seeing her. Rich didn't get it, and he'd once asked Carol what she thought the problem was.

"He thinks he's going to find another Kayla," she'd said.

That had been the start of one of their worst fights. Carol had no use for Martin just because he'd had a short affair when he and Kayla separated, but were not yet divorced. Rich once told Carol that Kayla used to cut Martin's hair and Carol often brought that detail up as an example of how Kayla had let Martin walk all over her. Carol didn't even *know* Kayla. If she did, Rich thought, she wouldn't be so eager to take sides.

Rich stopped at Bottles N' Bins on his way through Monterey and bought an off-brand Scotch that Martin liked. He used a pay phone to call Martin, and Martin told him he was no more than five minutes from his place. Martin said he'd be waiting in the parking lot.

·

WHEN HE GOT THERE Martin motioned him into the space next to his own car. "Neighbor never stays in town on weekends," he said when Rich got out. They hugged each other, and Rich poked Martin in the stomach.

"Look at this," he said. "You've put on some pounds."

Martin looked down at himself, as if the added weight was news to him. He laughed. "I guess I have," he said. Then he looked at Rich. "Still running?"

"Not much," Rich said. "Twenty, thirty miles a week."

Rich gave Martin the bottle of Scotch to carry and took his suitcase from the trunk. Sodium lights along the street began to flicker as they came to life. Martin led Rich up a flight of stairs, and when they came around a corner Rich was startled by the full moon rising over mountains to the east.

·

THE APARTMENT WAS FURNISHED with assorted pieces Martin said he'd found at yard sales. There was a brown plaid couch that someone's cat had clawed and a green vinyl reclining chair with duct tape on one arm. Rich set his suitcase on the floor beside a foot-high stack of newspapers—the *Wall Street Journal* and the Sunday *New York Times*.

"Sorry it's a mess," said Martin. "I meant to clean it up before you came."

"That's okay," Rich said. "Nice place."

Martin smiled. "$525 a month," he said. "Can you believe that?"

Rich didn't know if that was bad or good. "Amazing," he said.

Martin pulled the bottle from the bag. He put his chin to his chest and looked over his glasses to read the label. Rich remembered Martin's father making that same gesture, when they were in high school.

"Laphroaig," said Martin. "I used to drink this all the time."

Martin set the bottle on a bamboo coffee table and they looked at one another for a minute, smiling. Rich felt oddly, unexpectedly, that he was sorry he had come. Martin hadn't only put on weight, he'd aged, and Rich had been expecting him to look the same. "You're welcome," Rich said, feeling as he said it that these weren't the words he'd meant to say.

Rich said he could use a shower and Martin showed him where to find a towel. The back of the toilet was cluttered with bottles: vitamins and shampoo, Maalox, Pepto-Bismol, Cherry-Flavored Riopan. A wicker magazine rack overflowed with *Penthouse* and *Computer Age*. Rich pulled back the shower curtain to inspect the tub. A dry fern sitting on the tub enclosure's window sill released a few dead leaves.

He turned the water on and let it run while he undressed.

Martin was in bad shape; that was obvious. But Rich had seen him in bad shape before. After Kayla left, Martin had needed diversion more than anything, and Rich had done his best to fill up Martin's time. That winter they went twice a month to watch the Celtics and the Bruins play, and in the spring they'd spent a half a dozen evenings at Fenway. All the while he kept telling Martin Kayla's leaving was the best thing that could happen to him. She wasn't satisfied with Martin as he was; she had some idea of what he ought to be, and how she meant to go about effecting such a change. Kayla was a snob. Eventually, Martin came around to seeing it that way.

When Rich divorced his first wife, the year after, he and Martin had gone out to celebrate, finishing the evening in the Combat Zone, watching Princess Cheyenne at the Naked I. Rich remembered drinking vodka gimlets and proposing toasts to freedom, ex-wives and the aristocracy, by which he meant the Princess, and Martin's saying, "She's a goddamn artist. A goddamn artist."

·

RICH FELT BETTER, MORE alert, after he'd showered. He put on a clean pair of blue jeans and a polo shirt that had the logo of his company embroidered on the breast, above the heart. He had five more like it at home, because he liked the way they fit him. He'd been doing Nautilus and swimming, and he thought his arms and pecs looked fine. He didn't mind a shirt that showed that off.

When he came into the living room, he saw that Martin had set out soda water to mix with the Scotch. He'd also set out glasses and some ice cubes in a metal bowl. The LP playing on the stereo—Ben Webster and Coleman Hawkins—was a gift from Rich for Martin's birthday, several years before.

Martin didn't seem to notice Rich was there. He was

sitting on the sofa, a cigarette in one hand, his eyes closed, listening to "Tangerine."

"I thought you quit," said Rich.

"I did. More or less. I go through about a pack a month."

Rich sat down in the reclining chair and put some ice cubes in a glass. "Well, let me have one, then."

"No way."

"Sure. I mean it. I'm not about to sit here while you dissipate yourself alone."

Martin slid the pack across the coffee table. "How *is* Carol?"

"You know," Rich said, "Good and bad." He poured himself a Scotch. "Ashtray?"

Martin pointed to the kitchen. "Cabinet above the sink."

Rich had anticipated telling Martin all about it. How he and Carol seemed to argue even when they had agreed to make an effort not to. How their sex life wasn't great. How he sometimes spoke her name out loud, when he was alone, and how, no matter how he said it, however many times, it never sounded right. But Martin would just think that sounded crazy.

There were other things he wanted to tell Martin—about his job, his life, the way he often felt dissatisfaction gnawing at him. He wanted to tell Martin that he missed him, that he missed his one true friend.

When he came back from the kitchen with the ashtray, Martin tossed a book of matches to him. "Carol's good for you," he said.

"Right," said Rich. He splashed some soda in the glass of Scotch and lit his cigarette.

"You're more relaxed now than you used to be."

"I think that's jet lag."

"No, I mean it. I can tell she's made a difference for you."

Martin turned the record over. When Rich exhaled, the smoke came up and burned his eyes. Martin poured himself another Scotch and Rich held out his glass. "To dissipation," he said.

Martin saluted with his empty hand.

They listened to the record for a while, not talking, and Rich began to feel a little awkward, as if it was up to him to break the ice.

"So. California," he said.

"Yeah."

"It must be great. The weather. All those girls."

Martin looked at him with an expression Rich could not interpret.

"*Nude* beaches," Rich said. "Damn!"

"Jesus, Rich. It's way too cold for that."

"I only mean you have a certain number of advantages, that's all."

"Advantages?"

"To meet new people. Get out in the world and butt some heads."

Martin ground his cigarette into the ashtray and lighted another. "Boy," he said, "you haven't changed."

He smiled at Rich, as if he had meant to say that Rich was still the same old guy, the one he'd always known and loved, but it had not come out that way. Martin must have seen the quick emotion passing over Rich's face.

"You'd do great out here," said Martin. "You really would."

"Well, you will, too. I mean, you *have* done well."

"Look at you." He pointed to the embroidered logo on Rich's shirt. "Things like that."

"Like what?"

"What I mean is.... Well, I guess I mean you have a great

capacity for loyalty. You don't hold back. You go all out."

"It's just a shirt," Rich said.

"Well, isn't that the point? You're comfortable. You don't let small things bother you."

"What should I be bothered by?"

"I'm not accusing you of anything," said Martin. He stood, retrieved the pack of cigarettes, and sat back down. "Anyway," he said. "I have some news. Kayla and I may get back together."

Rich took another drag and blew the smoke out. "I didn't know you were in touch with her."

"We weren't until six months ago. She wrote to me, and we've been talking on the phone. I think she's changed."

"That's hard to know," Rich said. "Where is she, anyway? New Hampshire? I don't know that you can really tell a lot about somebody just from talking on the phone."

"Vermont," said Martin. "Maybe not."

Rich wanted to tell Martin that this sounded like a serious mistake. Wasn't this his friend? Wasn't he entitled to weigh in with what he thought? He had rights here. Not to mention obligations. He looked at Martin sitting on that ratty sofa, sucking tar into his lungs, and it seemed clear to him that he had obligations. "Doesn't work," he said.

"What doesn't work?"

"Trying to resuscitate a marriage."

"You may be right, Rich. I just know there's still some kind of bond with me and Kayla."

"Sure you feel a bond. Six long years of marriage. I'm not doubting some of them were good. It's the good times stay with you. Be careful."

"Well, I don't know if it's going to work out. And neither does Kayla. We're just talking about giving it a try."

Rich sat back and sipped his drink. He was thinking of an afternoon, many years before, when he'd come by to say hello, and all of them were sitting in the kitchen of the small apartment where Martin lived with Kayla when they first got married. It was the first hot day of summer, and they'd had the windows open. Rich drank beer, while Kayla snipped off strands of Martin's hair with barber's scissors. There were starlings gathered in a maple tree outside the kitchen window, and their chatter drowned out every other sound. Martin had his eyes closed, and there'd been a pause in which all three of them had seemed to listen. Kayla had set the scissors on the table, and put her hands on Martin's shoulders, and she'd looked up and smiled at Rich, and in the way her hands lay, in her smile, there was a tenderness, a purity of caring and intention, Rich had never seen in anybody else.

In that memory he loved them all, even himself, and he ached again, because he knew, as he'd known then, that everything would change.

He heard Martin say, "Goddamn," and looked over to see him brushing ashes off his trousers. "Anyway," Martin said, looking at him, "she's coming out for two weeks over Christmas."

"That's great," Rich said. "I hope it works out for you."

·

THEY WENT TO BED early because Rich said the trip had tired him, but when he lay down he had trouble sleeping.

The mattress on the sofa-bed was thin and he could feel the springs. Finally he got up and put the mattress on the floor. He drifted in and out of sleep, unable to relax. He kept thinking of the job he had to start on Monday, going through a checklist in his mind.

He began to dream about a train. Everything was dark,

and in the distance he could hear the train approaching. He couldn't tell if he was standing on the tracks. A horn blew, first a few short blasts and then a long one, rushing toward him. Then he was lying on his back, staring at the ceiling, and he could not remember where he was. He knew he'd had a nightmare. He turned over, and when he ran his hand across the pilled sheet he remembered: Martin's. California. Outside somewhere someone called a name.

He found his watch and pushed the dial light. It was seven-thirty his time. At home he would be getting up now, going for his run. He got up, went to the front door and opened it. The air outside was moist and salty. A thick fog had settled in, eerie in the street lights' orange glow. He stood there in his underwear, listening. Again he heard a shout, and someone else yelled back, "Go to bed!"

A car horn blared, and Rich recalled his dream. He closed the door. He thought the neighbor might have come home early and wanted in his parking space.

Rich put on his jeans and shirt and slipped his car keys in his pocket. When he stepped outside into the clammy, unfamiliar air he checked to make sure that the door would not lock after him.

The fog was thick enough he had to feel his way along the stair rail. When he reached the sidewalk he went slowly, testing with each step for solid ground. In a minute he was in the parking lot. Another step and he could no longer see the cars. There was no sound of any kind—no yelling, no horn. Was he the only one awake to see this? The fog was everywhere; he felt its moisture on his skin.

He listened to the rushing silence in his ears, hoping for a clue.

Traveler

The air has wrinkles in it. Things leak light. Nomi says, We need to get you glasses. I stared at Nomi's lamp. I tried to make it be still but I couldn't. I got dizzy. I tried to make the TV be still but first I sat down on the floor.

•

An ambulance came to our house. The sound it made was like a balloon that gets big then small. One man held the front door open while other men went in and out. I wanted to tell him not to let the flies in. I sat in the big chair in the den and watched. There was so much noise but I stayed very quiet. I watched the men. I tried to make them be still.

The men took Nomi. The ambulance sound got smaller. It was like a horn. Aunt Jem found me in the den. She is so fat it hurts her to walk. At her house she has a special chair with a handle she has to push to help her stand up. She sat on the couch. I thought, Oh no. We'll never get her back up.

•

Aunt Jem's house smells like weeds. She says I can sleep in Bob's room. Bob is far away he is a sailor. Aunt Jem has pictures of him in his sailor's costume. She has lots of pictures and a clock inside a jar with three gold balls that spin. She says, We'll have a talk now. Sit down. I sit in a rocking chair. She's in her big chair with the handle. Her face is very smooth. She says, You'll be my little boy now. I'll take care of you. You're brave. You'll be all right.

I look at the clock, the gold balls spinning. I don't want them to be still. Aunt Jem says, Go wash your face and hands and let's eat a bite. I've got fried chicken in there and banana cake.

•

My eyes have corners in them. If I hold my hand in front of me it disappears.

•

Aunt Jem tells me I can say grace if I want to and she will wait. I sleep in Bob's bed. I can hear the clock noise in the other room. I lick my hand and smell it.

•

Aunt Jem says, You'll like school. You'll have other children there. You'll have your teacher. But I don't want to go. I'm afraid. I look at Aunt Jem's smooth face but I have to look away to see her.

•

The man who lives next door comes over and we walk to school. He says he'll show me how to whistle like a mockingbird. He shows me but I can't. He says he will come to get me in the afternoon and we will try again.

•

The teacher gets mad. She says, Look at me. I look until I make her disappear and she says, That's right. Pay attention. Your Mama doesn't tell you look at people when they talk to you? I say, I am Aunt Jem's little boy now.

•

The mockingbird man is waiting on the grass. We hold hands. He says, What's the best thing you have ever eaten? I say pie. I try to look at him but we are walking too fast. He makes sounds like birds.

•

Aunt Jem goes across the street to use the telephone. I stay in the living room and watch the gold clock spin. It's very quiet. Maybe there is something in my eye. I can get it out. I look in the mirror but I can't see my eyes. My face is just a shape. I hold my hands in front of me and make them move like birds.

•

The mockingbird man brings a piece of pie for me and one for him. We sit on a bench and eat. When the bus comes we get on. He says, You don't have to go to school today. I'm happy. He makes bird sounds. A lady in a blue coat smiles at us. I try to make the bird sounds but I can't. He says, That's all right. We are going to a big park where there are lots of birds and they can teach you. I look out the window. I see green things moving, very fast. I say, My teacher gets mad. He says, You don't have to worry about her. My fingers smell like pie.

•

Aunt Jem says, Where did you go? I say, To the park. She says, No, that isn't right.

I stay quiet. She looks at me. I look straight ahead. I can see the little gold balls, flying. I can smell the weed smell. I feel hungry. Aunt Jem says, Tomorrow you will go to school. I'll get someone else to take you.

•

I can reach the latch on the screen door by standing on my toes. It's dark so I walk with my hand in front of me. I fall once. I find a street where there are buses and I wait. One comes. I get on. I put my quarter in the box and sit down by a window. Things outside turn blue. I hear a bird. I look out the window. Things move in and out where I can see them then I can't.

If they ask where I am going I will tell them I am going to a school where all the little boys have eyes like mine and I will whistle like a mockingbird and if they ask whose little boy I am I'll tell them Nomi's and if they ask my name I'll tell them Bob.

My Mother, Sewing

MY MOTHER, WHO HAS been dead fifteen years, is sewing in my living room. In life she never sewed but now, she says, she has the time.

"Here," she says, and makes room for me on the sofa. She sets aside the shirt she's mending and pulls a needle from the lapel of her winter coat. She threads the needle, holds it to my eye. I draw back.

"No," she says. "It's all right."

I lean toward her and she takes three quick stitches through the puffy flesh below my eye. There's no pain, but I feel the skin pulled tight by the thread. She breaks the thread with her teeth, then cuts the excess with nail clippers she's taken from her purse.

"There. That bag under your eye. It's gone."

In the mirror, I can see she's right. One side of my face is smooth.

"You look so old, Frank."

"I'm just tired, Ma. I just need to sleep."

"You were *always* tired," she says. "You *always* liked your sleep."

There are two faces in the mirror. One is my mother's.

"Here," she says, and holds the needle to the light. "Let me do the other one."

In the Catacombs of the Montresors

EVERY AUGUST, ON A still, hot afternoon when shrill cicadas clung, invisible, to cottonwoods, Mother would announce that we were going into town to buy my clothes for school. We always went to Hargreaves'. While Mother and Mrs. Hargreaves picked out jeans and shirts and underwear, I'd go to the back of the store and stand on the fluoroscope where I could press a black button and see my foot bones bunched up inside my shoes.

That summer I turned twelve. We were in Hargreaves' when Mrs. Appleton came in the door in her blue J.C. Penney's uniform and her bun coming undone and said, "Jack Rucker shot hisself this morning." She realized, when she'd said it, that she'd let herself sound pleased so she stopped short and, attempting to rewind the bun, said, "It's an awful thing. Just terrible."

"I declare," said Mrs. Hargreaves.

"Is he dead, Naomi?" Mother asked Mrs. Appleton.

"I expect he is," she said, and shook her head with such vigorous regret that the bun fell down again.

I felt a shiver of excitement. I had seen Jack Rucker only days before, walking on the other side of Main Street in his loose-fitting overalls and dilapidated canvas shoes. He'd taken off his railroad engineer's cap and wiped his forehead with it, revealing his dirty, yellow hair and leaving a black stripe above his eyebrows. This was the closest I had come to knowing someone dead.

There was a long moment of silence, during which Mrs. Appleton fished a handkerchief out of her pocket and practiced dabbing at the corner of her eyes. When she realized that we were waiting for the details, she leaned forward and said, in a church whisper, "Claudine came in to get a mattress pad and said that Dudley called before she left the house and told her." Claudine was married to Dudley Frierson, the Fletcher County sheriff.

"I can't imagine," Mrs. Hargreaves said.

"What did Claudine say *exactly*?" Mother asked. She pushed her glasses back up the bridge of her nose, the way she would when she intended to pay close attention. Whenever she did that with me, I knew I was in trouble.

"She said she thought she might as well come into town and get her errands done since Dudley couldn't make it home for lunch."

"I mean about Jack Rucker."

Mrs. Appleton leaned forward even more. "Dudley couldn't get home for lunch because he had to drive out to the Rucker place. Miss Izzard called and said she heard a gun go off, and she thought it either came from her pasture, in which case she wanted Dudley to come arrest whoever was trespassing on her land and scaring her milk cows, or else it came from Jack Rucker's and she didn't think he ought to be allowed to shoot off firearms that close to the road."

Mrs. Appleton straightened up, to catch her breath I thought, but after we had waited several moments, Mother said, "That's all?"

"Well. Yes," said Mrs. Appleton. She stood a little taller, as if to dodge the tone of Mother's question.

"I see what you're thinking, Miriam," she said to Mother, "but it doesn't take a lot of brains to figure out what happened. It's clear as day to me."

"Naomi," Mother said, "Miss Izzard's eighty-seven and

her hearing's not reliable. She could have heard the screen door slam or kids with firecrackers. Even if it was a gun there isn't any reason to think a thing like that."

"The man's wife ran off to *Abilene*! What other reason does he need?"

"Good Lord, Naomi. That was fifteen years ago."

Mrs. Appleton considered this, and said, "You might be right."

I hated to give in to disappointment, but I thought Mother was right, too.

Mother sighed. "I hope you haven't already told everyone in town Jack Rucker's dead."

"No. Claudine just this moment left the store."

"That's good," Mother said. "Better not to mention it to anybody else. If Jack Rucker were to hear he'd killed himself, I think he'd be annoyed."

·

FLETCHER, TEXAS WAS NOT a busy place in August. The marquee of the picture show said "CloSed U til SePt" and the yellowed sun blinds in the windows of the Green Stamp Redemption Center made the objects on display look like fossils caught in amber. The Paducah Rodeo was two months away, but the red and yellow poster from the year before was still taped inside the window of the barber shop, just below the coming season's high school football schedule.

A few old men and women stood in the shade of canvas awnings, fanning themselves with hats or handbags and watching the empty street as if they expected a parade to pass at any minute. Chester Bivens was the only person in the sun.

He sat behind a lopsided card table that had petitions spread across its top and a sign taped to the front that read "IMPEACH EARL WARREN."

"Hallo, Miriam! Hallo, Skipper!" he yelled to us. He was holding one of his petitions above his eyes, like a visor, and waving with his other hand for us to come across the street. We waved back, pretending we were in a hurry, but he put the petition down, cupped both hands around his mouth and yelled, "Come over here and say hello!"

Mother had the car door open on her side and I was setting the packages from Hargreaves' in the back.

"We'd better go say hi to Chester," she said.

Chester was editor-in-chief of the *Fletcher Index*, which meant he wrote the editorials and his grown son did the rest. Chester spent most of his time on the sidewalk outside the newspaper office, collecting signatures. He favored petitions aimed at local misbehavior, but in a dry spell he depended on Earl Warren.

"Miriam," he said, "you're prettier every time I see you. Hallo, Skipper." Chester thought, mistakenly, that I preferred this title to my name; it was intended to trick me into thinking he was friendly. "What's doing?"

"Buying school clothes," Mother said. "Summer goes by faster every year."

"Hmmm," said Chester. "Haven't noticed that myself."

He ran a spotted hand across his scalp and winked at me. I pretended not to see him do it, and stared, instead, at a brown tobacco stain on the front of his shirt. He saw what I was looking at and adjusted his suspenders to conceal it.

"What's this I hear about a ruckus at Jack Rucker's?"

Mother's glasses had slid down her nose. She pushed them back. "Has Naomi Appleton been over here?"

"Not this afternoon," said Chester. "Claudine Frierson said there were some goings on."

"I think she's just perturbed because Dudley isn't home for lunch."

"May be," Chester said. He rubbed his scalp again, as if he might find something he had lost up there. "But Dudley won't get down to work until Miss Izzard's fed him."

"Dudley isn't one to miss a meal," said Mother.

"That's an understatement," Chester said. "The man is more devoted to his gut than he is to keeping the peace."

Mother turned her head in the direction of the quiet street. "The peace pretty much keeps itself around here," she said.

"You might think so, Miriam, but there's a lot goes on. Something might need looking into that couldn't wait for Dudley to have seconds. We pay the man a full-time wage, we ought to get a full-time sheriff."

I thought I saw an editorial being born, but I was wrong; Chester was thinking something else entirely.

"Let me ask you something, Miriam," he said. "Would you vote for me for sheriff?"

Mother shifted on her feet. "Dudley's been sheriff a long time," she said.

"That's what *I* think," Chester said, and slapped the table with such force that one corner of the sign came loose. "You've proved my point. People just don't realize they're ready for a change until the opportunity presents itself."

•

"I DON'T KNOW WHY you told him that," I said when we were in the car.

"Told him what?"

"You'd vote for him for sheriff."

"I said no such thing."

"Well, you wouldn't, would you?" I asked. "If Chester was sheriff he'd close the picture show on Sundays."

"I don't think that's such a bad idea," she said. "The Sunday show's the same one you've already seen on Saturday."

"Anyway," I said, "Chester's too old to run for sheriff."

"I don't think he'll run. It's just another one of his ideas. He'll forget about it when the next idea comes along."

I put my cheek against the window and watched the white lines on the asphalt disappear beneath the car. When I closed one eye I could make them move the other way, so that it looked like we were firing tracer bullets. I moved my head until I got them lined up underneath the cross-bars of the hood medallion, and pretended I had locked my sights on Chester Bvivens.

•

WE LIVED WITH MY grandmother in the white, wood frame house where my mother had grown up. We moved to Fletcher when I was nine, after my parents divorced. Before that we lived in Galveston.

The house only had two bedrooms, but there was a small, enclosed porch in back that we'd fixed up for me. It wasn't insulated, so in winter I slept on the sofa in the living room. But from May until October, my bed and all my belongings— books, magazines, and a microscope that cost us fourteen books of Green Stamps—were out there and I felt I had a private world, far away from everything and everyone I knew. I had a lamp next to my bed and I'd often stay up reading after midnight while June bugs and candle moths sawed and fluttered at the screens.

I liked ghost stories. That summer I had read "The Cask of Amontillado," and was impressed and bothered by it in a way I wasn't used to. What happens in the story is the narrator, Montresor, gets revenge on a character named Fortunato by bricking him up inside the family catacombs of the Montresors.

Revenge appealed to me. But I was used to stories full of

severed limbs and ghastly apparitions, and this one, I thought, needed beefing up. There was a bit of screaming toward the end, but not enough. The story could have used a lot more of that kind of thing. I wondered why the author hadn't thought to have some rats sealed up inside the vault with Fortunato.

I often related stories I had read to my friend, Eugene Carr. When I told him the story of Montresor and Fortunato, I added the embellishments I thought it needed. He liked the story, too, and when I told him the parts I'd added he agreed it would be dull without them. But, unlike other stories we had liked and then forgotten, this story lent our friendship a shared wondering: What, we wondered, had Fortunato done to Montresor?

•

EUGENE SHOWED UP THE next morning, as he almost always did that summer, before I was out of bed. I awoke to a soft, steady tapping against the boards next to my pillow.

"Who's there?" I asked, already knowing the response.

"*The thousand injuries of Fortunato…,*" he said, in the lowest, most hollow voice he could manage.

Eugene waited with me in the kitchen while I ate a bowl of Froot Loops. The phone rang and I picked it up, but Mother picked up the extension in her bedroom at the same time, and said "Hello," before I had a chance to say a thing.

"What did I tell you?"

"Naomi?"

"I *knew* something bad was going on out there, and I was right."

"Going on out where?"

"Jack Rucker's, Miriam. Are you awake?"

"Yes, I'm awake, Naomi. I'm just used to hearing a hello when I pick up the phone."

"Hello," said Mrs. Appleton.

Mother sighed. "Naomi, what exactly is it that you called to tell me?"

"Jack Rucker's taken off. Dudley said there isn't any sign of him."

"Umm-hmmm," said Mother.

"He talked to Miss Izzard and she said she couldn't recall the last time she'd seen him."

"He might be on a trip."

"But *that's* the *thing*," said Mrs. Appleton. She paused. "That beat-up old Cadillac of his is sitting in the yard with the keys in the ignition. Dudley couldn't start it. He said the battery's bone dry."

"That *is* peculiar," Mother said. "What does Dudley think?"

"He's not overly concerned. Says no one's filed a report—not that there's anyone to do it—and he says he figures Jack is free to take off anytime he wants and where he's gone to isn't anybody's business but his own."

A customer must have come into Penney's, then, because Mrs. Appleton said, "I'll be right with you." But before she hung up she said, "I think he was abducted. That's my theory. That or Abilene."

•

I PUT THE PHONE down quietly and continued eating. I'd been eating slowly, anyway, and Eugene was fidgety; he'd started cracking his knuckles. Most people can crack their knuckles once and then they have to wait a while before they'll crack again, but Eugene could crack his just as often as he wanted. He could also crack his neck, and when he did you'd think he'd pulled his head out of its socket. It sounded like it hurt, but he said it didn't.

"If you keep doing that," I said, "your knuckles will swell up like golf balls."

"I wish they would," he said. "It'd be more interesting than watching you eat cereal."

I had four or five Froot Loops left, and I tried getting them to stay in the spoon without using the side of the bowl, but every time I brought the spoon up from underneath the milk they'd float away.

"The capillary effect," I said. I was going to explain this to Eugene while I had such a good illustration right there in front of us, but he groaned and twisted his neck around like he was going to crack it.

"OK," I said. "I'm done."

We went outside and settled on the porch steps.

Eugene said, "A bat got caught inside our swamp cooler yesterday."

"It did?"

"Yeah. My brother heard something flopping around inside so the dumbass pulled the vent off and the bat flew out and almost hit him in the face. It was flying around the living room, bumping into everything. My sister had a fit."

"Bats have radar," I said. "They don't bump into things."

"This one was drunk from being tumbled around inside the drum."

"What'd you do?"

"Smacked it with a broom," he said.

"Did you keep it?"

"Wanted to, but Mama said they carry rabies."

It was not yet ten o'clock, but the heat was bad already. If today was like the day before, we'd be in the hundreds before noon. The wind was coming through the yard in gusts and small red dust clouds hung above the road like smoke. A piece of cellophane hovered in a corner of the yard.

I told Eugene what I had heard, and asked if he thought Jack Rucker could have been abducted.

"Who'd want to kidnap *him*? Ain't nobody'd pay the ransom."

"Aliens," I said. "And don't say 'ain't'."

"What for?"

"Because it sounds dumb."

"You're the one who sounds dumb," Eugene said. "I meant the aliens. Why would aliens take J.R.?"

"I don't know," I said. "Experiments?"

I told Eugene what Mrs. Appleton had said the day before.

"That could be it," he said.

"But why would J.R. shoot himself?"

"I don't know," he said. He was urging a solitary ant into an ant lion's pit with the toe of his sneaker. "Guilty conscience?"

"What about?"

Eugene watched the trapped ant struggle to escape the pit. "Maybe Mrs. Rucker didn't run away to Abilene."

I pulled a blade of grass out of a crack between the steps and tried to see if I could whistle with it. There was some way you could hold it and whistle really loud, but I could never do it.

"Want to ride over to the park and watch the buffalo?"

Eugene groaned. "We always do that."

"Yeah," I said. I waited for Eugene's suggestion, but he just sat there. I knew what he was thinking. "You think Jack Rucker killed his wife?"

Eugene shrugged. "My dad says J.R. bootlegs liquor out of Oklahoma. Says he has a big stash hidden somewhere on his place."

"So?"

"So maybe Mrs. Rucker didn't like him doing it."

"So?"

Eugene turned his head, cracked his neck and smiled. "So J.R. could've read that story same as you," he said.

•

IT WAS FOUR MILES by the main road to the Rucker place, but if we went that way we'd have to pass Miss Izzard's. Instead, we rode our bikes out Cemetery Road, which wasn't paved, and skirted Miss Izzard's house. We were sweating by the time we got to J.R.'s, and we hadn't thought to carry any water. My mouth was dry and I could feel the dust between my teeth.

I'd snuck a flashlight out of the kitchen drawer, then we'd stopped by Eugene's house to get his Bowie knife. He said it would be useful for digging, and that it was a good idea to have a weapon in case Jack Rucker hadn't shot himself and caught us.

"If he did in Mrs. Rucker, there's no telling what he'd do to us," Eugene had said.

•

As WE MADE OUR way across a stubbled pasture to the house, I kept wishing Eugene hadn't said that. More than once I just about decided to turn back.

We stopped when we got close enough to read the numbers on the license plate of J.R.'s Cadillac. The elm tree in the front yard had been split by lightning years before, and afterwards the two halves grew in opposite directions, like they'd had a falling out. In the distance, I heard Miss Izzard's collie bark. When a grasshopper flew up from the grass and brushed my ear, I stumbled back and swatted at it frantically.

"*Quiet*," Eugene said.

The house was painted yellow, or it *had* been yellow before the sun and dust storms wore the paint down, leaving bare, gray boards exposed. Shingles had been beaten off the roof by hail and not replaced. The window screens had holes in them, as if someone inside the house had been shooting horse flies with a .22. It occurred to me that Jack Rucker looked as weathered as his house.

Beyond the battered rear end of the Cadillac, we could see the green, wooden door that covered the entrance to the storm cellar.

Eugene walked in that direction.

•

I saw no evidence that anyone had died in or was buried in the cellar, and I started to feel braver. I followed Eugene over to a cardboard box and watched him lift the flaps.

"Whiskey?"

"Old clothes and stuff," he said.

The cellar door creaked, and I thought it was the wind, but then I heard the sound of someone cough.

In that instant—frightened and surprised—I took a moment's satisfaction seeing Eugene's hands shake as he switched the flashlight off.

We concealed ourselves behind some boxes in the hollow underneath the stairs, and when the door came open and the top step groaned with someone's weight, it sounded like it had in every scary movie I had ever seen. I hoped I might pass out before I saw what made that noise.

We watched a flashlight's beam sweep over the walls and floor; whoever held the flashlight came down one more step and stopped. I expected, on the next step, I would see Jack Rucker's canvas shoes, but there was a second's pause and then a sneeze. It sounded like a woman.

I thought, then, that Mrs. Rucker had come back—and if she had, I hoped it was from Abilene.

Another quiet moment, then the woman blew her nose. The light appeared again, the visitor continued down the stairs, the cellar door fell shut. I prayed that Mrs. R. would turn around and go back up those stairs. But she continued down, and when she turned the flashlight towards us, and the light hit me in the eyes. I held up my hand up to my face to shield them.

She gave a little shriek and almost dropped the light. I grabbed hold of Eugene's arm, and when I did he screamed and then the woman screamed again. It was unsettling to hear all that screaming in that little cellar. I thought I might try getting out before she found me with the light again, but I wasn't sure where she was standing and didn't know if I could get between her and the stairs. I took my hand away to gauge my chances and when I did the light was in my eyes again.

"What on God's good earth are you doing over there?" said Mrs. Appleton. "You scared me half to death."

My mouth was so dry that the insides of my cheeks were stuck to my gums. I tried to speak, but all I managed was a hiccup. Mrs. Appleton looked at Eugene.

"Get up out of there," she said to him, "and tell me what you think you're doing."

Eugene said, "We were riding bikes and stopped to rest a while."

"In the *storm cellar?*"

"We thought it would be cooler down here," he said. "We're sorry if we scared you."

"You certainly did," said Mrs. Appleton, and laid her hand dramatically over the little oval name patch on her J.C. Penney's uniform. "What if I had a weak heart?"

"Sorry," Eugene said again.

We stood there for a while, not speaking, until we all began to feel uncomfortable. Eugene said he thought we needed to be getting on, and just about that time the door came open once again and someone yelled, "Come on out of there and dvon't try anything. I'm armed!"

Mrs. Appleton stepped over to the stairs and squinted into the sunlight. "Chester?"

"You all right, Naomi?" I heard Chester say.

"Good enough," she said, "for having had the wits scared out of me."

•

I LET MRS. APPLETON go up the stairs first, since I thought Chester would be less likely to shoot her by mistake. But when I got outside I saw Chester standing to one side with a tire tool in his hand. I guess he'd planned on knocking us over the head with it when we came out.

"What are you doing out here, Naomi?" he asked.

"I was worried about Jack Rucker," she said. "I thought he might be lying out here injured and no one else to help him."

"The boys come with you?"

Eugene said, "We rode our bikes."

"What was all that screaming?" Chester asked. "I saw your car, Naomi, and thought you might be getting murdered down there."

Mrs. Appleton looked sheepish, and Eugene was studying the ground, so I tried my voice again and found I'd got it back. I said, "We wanted to see if we could get an echo."

"An echo?"

"Sure. A small chamber like that sometimes produces interesting acoustics."

Chester looked skeptical, but before he could pursue the matter Mrs. Appleton said, "What brings *you* out here?"

"I just thought I'd have a look around," he said. "Sheriff

down in Waco called Dudley to let him know Jack Rucker's coming in to Fletcher on the 4:10 Trailways. Jack was trying to hitch a ride on 287."

"Thank heaven he's all right," said Mrs. Appleton, and covered her name patch with her hand again. I let loose another hiccup.

There was a noise then, like a shot, and my first thought was to hit the dirt. I was glad I didn't, though, because I would have been the only one who did. The shot had come from the direction of the Cadillac. We walked over there. I thought a tire might have blown. But the tires looked fine.

Chester said, "This might be what I heard about," and got the keys from the ignition.

We gathered around the trunk while Chester fumbled with the keys. When he finally got the trunk to open, it was like an oven's heat had been released. We all stepped back. Inside, I saw a wooden case of R.C. Cola, or what was left of it. Several bottles had exploded and the shards of glass were scattered in the bottom of the trunk.

Chester wiped his forehead with his sleeve and shut the lid. He stood there for a while, jangling the keys in one hand and looking up and down the road as if he might decide to take it somewhere besides Fletcher. Maybe he was thinking J.R. had the right idea.

Eugene and Mrs. Appleton and I stood waiting, as if we knew what we were waiting for, and no one said a thing. I began to think about the long ride home along that dusty road.

Chester cleared his throat. "Let's not let your mama know about this, Skipper," he said.

I had no intention of telling Mother where I'd been, and I would have said "OK" to Chester, except a hiccup stopped me and then, for some reason, I decided it was better not to say it after all. I looked across the pasture, where we'd left our bikes, and saw a wall of storm clouds coming towards us from the west.

Mrs. Appleton said, "We could get tornadoes out of that." They didn't look that bad to me. But I said, "Yes, we could."

"Hail, at any rate," she said. She sounded pleased.

Liebfraumilch

IN MY FAMILY WE named our pets for liquor. We had dogs named Brandy and Tequila. We had a cat named Vodka, to whom I was allergic. We even had a mynah bird once, for a short while, who we called Johnnie Walker.

Vodka died one Christmas while we were away, visiting my grandparents. The neighbor found her, wrapped her in a plastic bag and put her in our freezer where she stayed until the ground was soft enough, in spring, to bury her. One night I found my sister out there in the garage, standing in her nightgown with the freezer door wide open, looking in on Vodka. It was weird, my sister standing in the freezer light, her breath making clouds. "Victoria?" I whispered, "Vicky?" But if she heard me she didn't turn around. I went back to bed and left her there.

That was our last winter in Amarillo. We moved that June to Las Vegas, where my father had been hired to be the comptroller of a private hospital just a few blocks off the Strip. Famous people used to come there sometimes: entertainers. I realize, now, that most of them were there for plastic surgery or de-tox, but my father never mentioned anything about their illness. He'd just say that so-and-so had checked in for a few days, and he'd pass on to us the opinion of the staff; this one was a prima donna, that other one was down to earth.

I wondered what words the staff used to describe my father. "Exacting" was the word my mother favored. "Your father's an *exacting* man," she'd tell us over dinner, arching one eyebrow ironically to let us know that she meant more than she was saying. This was her response to any incidental criticism he might level at her, or at us, ranging from the price or tenderness of that night's pork chops to the quality of Vicky's posture at the table, to my imperfect grammar. My mother's arched eyebrow was shorthand and we took its meaning: I am not wounded by such criticisms, and you should not feel wounded, either.

"Guilty as charged," my father would say, every time. "Now tell me, judge. Where might I go to pay my fine?"

She would tap the corner of her mouth with one long, painted fingernail, and he would get up, walk around the table and kiss her, very formally, on that spot.

My father wasn't handsome, but he had winning ways. People should have been intimidated by his size—six-feet-two, 280 pounds—but there was something in his bearing or expression that made strangers walk right up to him and start conversations. I saw this happen all my life, in grocery stores and banks, in movie theaters and airports. They would tell him things about themselves, and he would listen as if this was what he'd come there for, to hear them talk about their stiff joints or their bunions, their lost opportunities, their piddling triumphs, their troubles with their wives or kids, or with the law.

With women he was sly and courtly, giving them the Full On Treatment, as my mother called it, bearing down on them with all of his considerable charm. Women seemed to recognize that this was ceremony, not seduction, and most were glad to play along, teasing him or turning diffident, taking on the role of temptress or coquette, looking up at him from hooded eyes, provocative or pure-as-driven. He did not discriminate between the pretty women and the plain ones. I once saw him sweep a ninety-year-old woman off her feet, at her birthday party. He held her close and danced her through the tables in the banquet room of the Red Barn, in Amarillo, singing "Star Dust" in her ear until the record on the jukebox ran out. Then he walked her back to her chair with his arm around her waist, and before she sat down she turned and kissed him on the cheek. You could see from twenty feet away that she was blushing.

At work, my father was all business. In his pressed white half-sleeve shirts and narrow dark ties, his creased trousers, he embodied the idea of the perfectly straight line. He kept his fingernails cut close and straight across, his sideburns squared off at his temples. The hair on the back of his head appeared to have been trained to stop growing two inches above his collar. In the pockets of his shirts he carried scraps of paper on which he had made lists, in pencil, and his letters were precise and angular, almost cuneiform. They looked like the tracks that certain beetles leave in sand.

I think about the sound my father's hard-soled shoes made, coming down the hospital's waxed corridors. My father spent his life in hospitals, and probably grew deaf to that sound, but it was part of him, an attribute that adheres permanently to my image of him, and that makes me wonder how much of what surrounds us we take on, how much of it *becomes* us without our knowing?

•

VICKY TURNED FIFTEEN THAT summer and my parents wanted to do something special for her birthday. My mother made dinner reservations at the Rathskeller, a place someone had recommended to my father where the waitresses dressed up as fräulein and the beer was served in steins.

My father came home late that Friday afternoon. Mom had been fretting for an hour by the time we heard his car pull in the driveway.

She had tried to calm herself by settling on the sofa with a glass of rosé and a copy of *House Beautiful*, but after half an hour had gone by, she set the magazine back in the wicker rack next to the coffee table, sipped her wine and stared out the front window. When we heard the car, she stood up. But instead of throwing open the front door and yelling out to him that we were late, as I'd expected her to do, she went down the hallway to her bedroom, saying she was going to put on her lipstick.

I went to get my suit coat from my bedroom, but I stopped in the hallway when I heard my father come through the front door. I turned to see him shimmying across the living room, away from me, his jacket half off. His head was down and he was holding a plastic go-cup in his left hand. He was taking his time, moving to some sad and soulful music only he could hear. He stopped in the dining room to set the cup down on the table and to drop his jacket on a chair. Then he disappeared into the kitchen.

"Are we ratty?" he yelled.

"Hell, yes," Mom yelled back. "We've been ready for an hour."

"Round 'em up, then!"

I picked my suit coat off my bed and carried it into the kitchen, where I sat down at the breakfast bar and watched Dad pour beer into a frosted mug he'd taken from the freezer. He put tomato juice, Tabasco and black pepper in the beer, and stirred it with a butter knife that happened to be lying on the counter. When he turned around, he grinned and winked at me.

"Want one, Russ?" he said, and held the mug out, "Special occasion."

I would have taken a plain beer, but bloody beer did not

appeal to me. "I don't think so, Dad," I said, "Thanks anyway."

He leaned back against the counter and drank half the beer in one long swallow. Then he held it out to me again, offering the rest with an expression that said, Are you sure? I shook my head.

He finished the beer and set the mug in the sink. "*Vamanos!*" he yelled.

Mom had stopped in the dining room to hang Dad's jacket on the back of the chair, and to pick up the go-cup he'd left sitting on the table. She had on a blue silk evening dress and heels. Earlier that day she'd done her hair up in a chignon, and put on the dangling silver earrings that my father had brought back for her from Mexico.

"Mercy!" Dad said. He stepped back and turned his head to look at her out of the corners of his eyes, as if the sight of her head-on might blind him. "You're not worried that you'll make the other women jealous?"

"You're not worried that you'll have to fend off other men?" She had to reach around him to empty the cup in the sink, and when she did he put an arm around her waist, leaned down and kissed the back of her neck. She straightened and turned to peck him on the cheek, then used her thumb to rub off the spot of lipstick she had left there. She was frowning as she did it.

Vicky was standing in the dining room by then, not saying anything, just waiting for us to admire her. She had on a sleeveless dress that was the pale green color of the melon daiquiris my mother sometimes made and sipped beside the pool. The dress showed off her figure. She'd put on the tennis bracelet Dad had given her the Christmas before last. I thought that was smooth of her, to wear that bracelet for Dad's benefit, even though I knew she didn't really like it.

Vicky had my mother's lightly-freckled skin, her blue eyes and auburn hair. Even I could see she was a knockout in that dress.

Dad walked over, put his arm around her shoulder and gave her a squeeze. "I can't believe my baby's turning fifteen," he said.

•

AT THE RESTAURANT, DAD had our station wagon valeted and then held the door for us and ushered us inside as if he were the maitre d'. We went down a flight of stairs and waited just inside the door while Dad went up to find the hostess.

"Warm in here," Mom said, as we waited.

It was stifling. I could feel myself begin to sweat under my suit coat, and I longed to shed my tie. A couple who'd come in the door behind us waited half a minute, then left. Vicky pulled a *Nifty Nickel* from a rack next to the door and started to fan herself with it, but Mom looked at her severely and she put it back.

People in the restaurant looked up when we came in. We were clearly overdressed. The place was loud and lit up like a stadium; the tables were uncovered and the light reflecting off their polished surfaces came at you like a set of high beams in a rearview mirror. Waitresses were shouting orders to the barman as they pushed their backsides through the swinging kitchen doors, and every time the doors swung open I could hear the sound of metal being tortured with a saw. Six or seven football players from the university were drinking beer from yard-long glasses at the bar, and one of them said "hoo-*eee*" as my mother and my sister passed.

"This is nice," my mother said, as she sat down. She set her clutch bag on the table and turned in her chair to give herself a better view. Her expression was one of alert curiosity, as if she were taking in the customs of an unfamiliar country, where they did things differently: let the chimpanzees drive buses, maybe, or turn pigs loose in museums. My mother was a former court reporter and she retained a repertoire of such expressions from her working days, when it had been professional necessity to be able to look studious, or totally impartial, or just bored, while taking down the most depraved details of criminal behavior.

My father held my sister's chair for her then sat down. "How about champagne?" he said, looking for a waitress.

Vicky was squinting to see past me to the bar. She was getting contacts for her birthday, but they hadn't come in yet and she had left her glasses home, out of vanity. Suddenly her ears and neck flushed scarlet and she looked away. I turned around to see the football players doubled over, laughing. One looked up and saw me staring at him; he puckered up and kissed the air, obscenely, and the others roared approval.

Mom turned in her chair to face us. "I don't know," she said. "Maybe we should go to the Great Wall."

"They don't have champagne at the Great Wall," Dad said. "Besides, I thought we wanted something special."

"I want to stay here," Vicky said. "I think it's fun."

A waitress came up to our table, then, and stood there glumly, waiting for our order. Her short, black hair was plastered to her forehead, and her eye makeup had smeared. The Heidi outfit she had on was way too big for her; its puffy shoulders fell around her biceps, and the bodice sagged.

"We'd like to start with champagne," Dad said.

She looked up and glanced around the table, as if she was just now seeing us. What she saw appeared to make her tired. "No champagne," she said. "Beer and cocktail. Wine. Aperitif."

"No champagne?" my father asked.

"Sorry," said the waitress.

Dad shook his head, disbelieving. "Well I'm a sad man," he said.

"Is the air conditioning out?" Mom asked. "It's awfully hot in here."

"Whole thing go this afternoon," the waitress said. "They say whole unit need replace. Guys work on it now."

The kitchen doors swung open and we heard wrecking yard sounds, like whole cars being fed into a crusher. Someone back there yelled, "*Go fuck your mother, Gino!*"

Dad slipped a hand into his jacket pocket and removed a folded twenty-dollar bill. He held it out to the waitress between the knuckles of his first two fingers. "Maybe you could send someone to find champagne for us?" he said, winking at her. "It's my daughter's birthday."

The waitress scowled. "Who'm I send?" she said. "Maybe Chef can fetch for you? I go ask him. He no very busy right now."

My father's face fell. He put the bill back in his pocket and said, "Wine, then." Before he could say more, she turned to leave. "Don't I get a choice?" he shouted after her.

She turned around. "Liebfraumilch," she said.

My father raised his hands in resignation. "Shame about that dress," he said, when she had gone. "Made to handle a full house and all she's holding is a low pair."

"Can I take my jacket off?" I asked.

"I can't believe they don't have champagne," Vicky said.

"I can," Mom said, primly. "Frankly, I'm surprised they let the patrons eat off plates. It might be more efficient to just line us up at troughs."

The waitress came back with an open bottle of Blue Nun

and set it on the table without bothering to pour. She took our order and then headed to the bar, ignoring the people at a nearby table who were trying urgently to flag her down.

Dad poured the wine and then made toasts. He wished Vicky happy birthday, and we toasted her, and then he toasted Mom for having the good sense to be good looking, and then he toasted her genes and the good job she'd done passing all her pretty chromosomes on to her daughter. The wine was syrupy and not that cold. I raised my glass and held it to my mouth, but after that first sip I knew I didn't want another. Everybody else went through theirs like it was the best thing they had ever tasted.

Dad looked at me. His eyes were dreamy. "Russ," he said, "Son?" He was holding up his glass as if he'd just discovered it was there.

"Yeah, Dad?"

"You know what we are, don't you? You and me?"

I shook my head.

He smiled, sadly. "Partners," he said. "*Compañeros.*"

He reached across the table and patted my cheek. Then he poured more wine and lifted his glass for a final toast.

"To my family," he said. Tears filled the corners of his eyes.

When the salads came Dad told the waitress that we'd like another bottle. I asked for a Coke, and Mom asked how the air conditioning repair was coming. The waitress said she thought they'd have it back on pretty soon and Mom said how soon, and the waitress shrugged and hurried off.

Vicky stood up and excused herself. She tacked towards the ladies room, avoiding the direct and obvious route so that the football players at the bar would get a chance to take a good long look at her.

"All I can say," Mom said, "is that they'd better get that air conditioning back on soon, or half the room is going to go into heat prostration."

We picked at our salads and the waitress brought the second bottle of Blue Nun, but forgot to bring my Coke, and Mom asked if we couldn't get a round of ice waters, and then a man at the next table started to complain that he'd been waiting half an hour for his entrée, and it shouldn't take that long considering he'd only ordered sauerbraten. Our waitress listened with a kind of Joan-of-Arc expression on her face, nodding vaguely with her eyes fixed to the ceiling as if she were just that moment getting new instructions about how best to rout the English.

She went towards the kitchen, but I watched her veer off before she got there. She went past the bandstand, where a man in lederhosen and Tyrolean hat was removing an accordion from its case. She skirted the tables without looking at them, like a blind person who's memorized where every piece of furniture sits in a room. As she passed the hostess station and the register, then ducked through the velvet curtain that was draped across the entryway, the accordion player launched into "Bad, Bad Leroy Brown." The waitress was still carrying her order pad in one hand. The last glimpse I had was of her thin calves working their way up the stairs.

•

"Where *is* our waitress?" Mom asked, scanning the room.

Dad refilled the glasses; the second bottle of Blue Nun was nearly empty. We'd been finished with our salads for a quarter hour.

"I think she left," I said.

The accordion player was so loud the stemware rattled in the rack above the bar. A table of Midwestern-looking tourists near the bandstand stomped their feet and clapped along.

"That's it, then," Mom said. "If I stay here another minute, I'll pass out." She set her napkin on her salad plate and pushed back her chair.

Dad looked once around the room, hopefully, as if our dinner might just then be coming to our table. Then he sighed and stood up. "Okay," he said. "I'll just make a pit stop."

He headed off in the direction of the men's room, listing to his port side as he went.

Just then, the biggest of the football players came over to our table.

"Hi," he said, to Vicky.

Vicky smiled at him with just her top teeth showing, the way I'm sure some magazine had told her was sophisticated. She had probably spent hours in her bedroom practicing that smile.

"That your dad?" he said, pointing with his chin.

"Yes," Vicky said.

Mom was staring at the football player.

The player pushed his lower lip out. "My friends and I were wondering," he said, "if those are real." He pointed with his chin at Vicky's chest.

"*What?*" Mom asked. She said it as if she had not heard, which was entirely possible, the music being what it was.

"Well," he went on, smiling innocently at my mother, and speaking louder, as if for her benefit. "We kind of have a bet on."

Mom stood up. In her heels, she came up to about his Adam's apple. "You go back and join your other ill-behaved friends now," she said. "If I have to call the manager, I will."

The football player shrugged. "That would be Raimundo," he said. "I can call him for you if you want. Ray's a good guy." He let his eyes drop to my mother's chest, and left them there a moment. Then he walked back over to his buddies at the bar.

Mom picked her purse up off the floor. "Get up," she said. "We're leaving. *Now*. Russ, go find your father."

·

THERE WAS ONLY ONE stall in the men's room, and the door was closed.

"Dad?" I called. I could see his shoes, so I knew he had to be in there. "We're going, Dad," I said. "Come on."

I heard him moan.

"Come on, Dad," I said. "Time to load up." I rattled the stall door, but he had put the lock on.

There were three quick knocks on the outside door, and Mom stuck her head in. "What is taking so long?" she asked.

"I can't get him out of there," I said.

She came in the men's room and stood at the stall door. "Come on, sweetheart," she said. "Time to go."

We heard movement, then the lock turned. The door swung open, and I saw Dad sitting on the toilet cover, leaning back against the wall with one hand on his forehead. It took a while to get him on his feet. He kept saying he just wanted to lie down.

"We're going home, now," Mom said. "You can lie down in the car."

I was wondering how we were going to get him across that crowded restaurant, and up those stairs. He was heavy, and if he passed out on us, we would never budge him.

Vicky was sitting at our table, drinking what was left of the wine. She stood up when she saw us, took two steps in our direction, and fainted.

"Oh, for Christ's sake," Mom said.

We pulled out a chair from a nearby table, put Dad in it

and went over to where Vicky had collapsed. People at the tables all around us were just staring, as if we were the floor show. The accordion player hadn't let up; the Midwestern tourists were clapping to "Brown Sugar."

Mom borrowed a glass of water and a napkin from the nearest table, and she managed to get Vicky sitting up. She dipped a corner of the napkin in the water and dabbed Vicky's face with it.

"Come on, baby," Mom said. "You just got too hot. Get up. Let's get out of here."

I looked up and saw the football player standing over us. "She all right?" he asked.

"She'll be fine," Mom said. "Now why don't you and your friends do something useful and help me get my husband up those stairs?"

•

THERE WAS A BENCH out front, beneath the portico, and we laid my father out on it and waited for the station wagon to appear. Mom patted down Dad's pockets and came up with the twenty he had offered to the waitress. She thanked the football players, who were standing around us looking sheepish, and told them we could take it from there. When the car came she handed the money to the valet guy and he helped us get my father in the back. We couldn't get him all the way in; he was too tall, and his feet stuck out. It seemed futile to try to move him any farther, so we rolled the window down, lifted up his legs, and closed the tailgate. Then we set his feet down on the window ledge. I made sure the latch was fastened while Mom removed Dad's shoes and tossed them in the back, beside him. I knew she didn't want them to fall off on our way home.

I saw, then, that the wine had gone to her head, too. I'd been fooled by her expression, which was sober as a deacon's, and by the steadiness in her voice as she'd helped coax my father up the stairs. Now I saw her sway, just slightly, as if she were standing on a dock rocked gently by a distant speedboat's wake. She put one hand against the car to steady herself, and leaned down to take off her high heels. When she stood up again I was surprised how suddenly diminished she seemed, standing in her stocking feet.

She looked at Vicky, then at me. Vicky had mascara running down her cheeks; she was squinting at us as if we were fifty yards away, not standing right in front of her.

"You drive," Mom said, handing me the keys.

I was thirteen years old, and the only cars I'd ever driven were the go-carts at a miniature golf course outside Amarillo, but neither Vicky nor I argued with her. Vicky got into the back seat and I slid in behind the wheel. Mom walked around the front of the car and got in the other side. After I had moved the seat up, Mom said, "Check your mirrors," and I rolled the window down and adjusted the side view mirror; then I turned the rearview mirror so I could see out the back. My father's legs obscured my view, the way they stuck out of the tailgate window, but there was nothing we could do about that.

I fit the key in the ignition, turned it, and the engine started right away. I put my seat belt on and waited for instructions.

"Put your foot on the brake," Mom said. "Good. Now move the gear shift to the 'D'."

I did as she said, and when I took my foot off the brake we started rolling forward. We hit a speed bump and the station wagon lurched to one side. That took me by surprise and I let go of the steering wheel.

Mom leaned over, took the wheel, and steered us expertly

around one of the columns holding up the portico. I found the brake again and stopped us.

"Lesson Number One," Mom said. "Never let go of the wheel."

"Maybe you should drive," I said.

She looked at me, her eyes narrowed. "No," she said, after a moment. "You can do this."

I gripped the wheel more tightly this time, made a wide turn in the parking lot, and brought the car back to the street.

"Turn your signal on," Mom said. We waited while the cars sped past on Pecos Boulevard. "Go on, now," she said. "Ease out there. We don't have all night."

When I saw a gap I punched the pedal, too hard, and we shot out of the driveway into the middle lane. A taxi swerved to miss us, laying into his horn at the same time. I turned the wheel back to the right, too sharply, and we rode up the curb onto the restaurant's grass. I took my foot off the accelerator and we stopped again. I could feel my heart going in my chest.

"Way to go, Mario," Vicky said.

Mom shot her a withering look. "That's all right," she said to me. "You're doing fine."

She took the wheel with one hand, straightened it and told me to put my foot back on the gas pedal. I took the wheel from her, pushed the pedal down, more gently this time, and we moved slowly forward, off the grass and curb and back into the street. I stayed in the right-hand lane, going fifteen miles an hour while I got the feel of the accelerator. Other drivers honked as they whipped past, but I ignored them. I was concentrating on not letting go of the wheel, and on giving her the right amount of gas.

At the next light, which was Desert Inn, I turned right. I got it better that time, keeping us in the same lane, straightening her out. I felt a whole lot calmer, having made that turn, and now I started to enjoy what I was doing. I had been holding onto the wheel so tightly that my hands hurt, but now I made myself relax my grip. It surprised me how a big car like that would respond to such a small amount of pressure. I experimented with the steering, moving the wheel slightly to the right and to the left, bringing us back steady, straight and true. I took my right foot off the gas pedal and tapped the brake with my left, making the car slow; I put my foot back on the gas and accelerated smoothly. I took it up to thirty-five and held it there.

The temperature had dropped now that the sun was down, and the cool air coming through the open tailgate window smelled of wet lawns and of sage and creosote: smells of summer, and the desert all around us. The outline of the Charleston Range was barely visible against a blue and salmon sky, a ragged line from which the black backdrop of mountains seemed to hang. The cool air felt like heaven, after the hot restaurant. My father had begun to moan.

Mom looked over the back seat. "If you need to throw up," she said, "we'll pull over."

Desert Inn merged with the Strip a few blocks later. I came around the curve and waited with my blinker on, as Mom had told me, and then, when my chance came, I pulled into traffic. I was feeling sure now of my driving skill, confident of my ability to handle our big wagon. I felt in command of all the mechanisms; I was driving like a pro.

Dad had gone quiet again. I figured he'd passed out and we would not be pulling over, so I put my blinker on and moved into the center lane. Mom had stopped watching me. She was sitting back now, with her eyes closed, one hand resting on the clutch bag in her lap. The other hand was lying on the seat beside her, her silver earrings nestled in her open palm.

Traffic on a Friday night was heavy and we crept along with it in the direction of downtown. We went past the Algiers and the Sands, the Stardust, the Frontier, the Thunderbird, the Riviera. There were smaller hotels and casinos tucked between the big ones, their marquees advertising nickel beer and twenty-five cent hot dogs, double odds on craps, and Paycheck Poker. We passed wedding chapels, souvenir shops, liquor stores and drive-through donut franchises, all of them lit up like movie sets. Even the McDonald's sign was dressed up like a Vegas showgirl, its golden arches made up of a shimmering cascade of yellow lights.

I glanced in the side view mirror and saw Vicky's profile; she was looking out, impassive, at the parade of wonders, almost regal in her unconcern.

No one on the Strip took any notice of a thirteen-year-old boy behind the wheel of a big station wagon. Everything on every side was meant to make you look up: the enormous marquees with their fifteen-foot-tall letters, their lights sparkling; the hotels with searchlights going in their parking lots. The scale of things was meant to make you feel small, but I felt a thrill in being overwhelmed by it, of being made invisible. I understood that skyline in a way I hadn't until then—the way it let you lose sight of the ordinary, human-sized events that made up your own life; the way the lightscape let you hide your sameness, even from yourself.

Compared to all this, I was unremarkable. But I did not feel small, or insignificant. I was carrying my family home, through danger, in a foreign place. I sat up straighter and leaned into the wheel, my fingers nestled in its molded ridges, my grasp relaxed and sure. The gleaming, long hood of the car reflected all the lights of the marquees, the way a clear, smooth lake reflects Orion on a summer's night. I looked past that to the road beyond, to where I was heading. I kept my eyes fixed to the painted lines on the black pavement and steered cautiously between them, mindful of the many hidden obstacles on which we might run aground.

Acknowledgments

I am grateful to teachers, colleagues and friends who read early drafts and provided thoughtful criticisms that helped to make these stories better. Among them: John L'Heureux, Nancy Packer, Erin McGraw and Brent Spencer.

The late Leonard Michaels gave me encouragement at a time when I most needed it.

Respect, and gratitude, to Lorrie Moore.

I am fortunate to have been afforded uninterrupted time to write by the creative writing programs at Stanford University and the University of Wisconsin-Madison, as well as the Djerassi Resident Artists Program in Woodside, California.

My wife, Alka Joshi, has supported, encouraged and inspired me. Her astonishing determination, and the remarkable range of her talents, reminds me daily that an artist can accomplish much, and overcome much, through purpose, perseverance, and audacity.

About the Author

BRADLEY JAY OWENS grew up in the Texas Panhandle. He is a former journalist and Foreign Service officer who served in Washington, D.C. and Port-au-Prince, Haïti. His stories and essays have appeared in *Ploughshares*, *The Threepenny Review*, *The Henfield Prize Stories*, *The Christian Science Monitor* and elsewhere. He has received the Henfield Prize, the National Prize in Fiction from The Loft Literary Center, and fellowships from the University of Wisconsin-Madison and the Cité Internationale des Arts. He lives in Pacific Grove, California. For more information, go to bradleyjayowens.com.

CPSIA information can be obtained
at www.ICGtesting.com
Printed in the USA
LVHW091652180821
695554LV00008B/1049